Tales from
The Widow's Walk

MICKOE

Tales from
The Widow's Walk
c/o The Bronx

by Danny Hofer

All characters appearing in this work are fictitious. Any resemblance to persons, living or dead, is purely coincidental. The places, companies, organizations, and events depicted herein are fictitious. No association with any real place, company, organization, or event is intended or should be inferred.

copyright © 2020 by Danny Hofer
All rights reserved. No part of this book may be reproduced, scanned, or distributed in any printed or electronic form without written permission.
First Edition: January 2020
Printed in the United States of America

To my wife Claire.

It's been 40 years together and our love strengthens by the day.

You are the anchor of our family and have given me the greatest gift of my life, our son Daniel.

40 YEARS Together

Contents

Introduction
The Cardboard Kids

Being born in the Bronx in 1945 and living there in the fifties, sixties, and seventies, made me realize just how unique and mystical this piece of God's realm truly was. Unique in not realizing that we were actually working poor, as opposed to the societal definition bequeath to our people as being middle class. We were the youthful army that put cardboard in our shoes and sneakers, a result of having only one pair of each for the entire year. We had two pair of dungarees and school pants riddled with patches so that they could survive the year also. Our recreation saw us going down sewers to retrieve the only Spaldeen, which enabled the stick-ball game to continue.

All our mothers went out daily with their pull carts and hunted out the various sales, even if it involved a mile trek. Our world was one of tuna-fish and egg-salad sandwiches. Ham was an extravagance never to be had, replaced by bologna and peanut-butter-and-jelly sandwiches. These were just a few of a long list of deprivations we endured, but it defined a universality that bound all of us together. A happy army of young Bronx-ites, not having material treats others had, but never realizing that fact and, as a result, enjoying our environs and looking forward to each and every day we could play in the schoolyard.

1

Another unusual quality, which could be seen in the neighborhood, was defined by its somewhat abrasive, blue-collar humor that emanated from the schoolyard to the many bars sprinkled throughout the neighborhood. Why unusual? Because it transcended any comical situation that I have experienced throughout my life. A humor that was forged from generations of people originating from the streets with the unknown realization that we were two levels above destitution.

1
The Hat

It was February of 1970 and the Duke, while having his coffee, just stared at the hat. All during that winter, this hat hung daily on the same hook at Duke's bar, The Widow's Walk.

Duke Callahan was a strong male specimen at six-foot-one with black hair and dark eyes that had a devilish twinkle which coupled with his mischievous smile. Duke had a loving, adversarial relationship with Jimmy Logan. For years Logan worked as Duke's steady, day bartender. Many a night after Logan's shift, they both would enjoy a steak and over imbibe at one of the Bronx's many restaurants.

Now, however, the Duke was obsessed with Logan's hat.

Duke says, "Jimmy could you get some ice from the back? Do you want a sandwich when I get back?"

Logan's five-foot-eight frame was topped by a tiny head which was now crimson.

"You know you're an asshole. Why didn't you get the ice when you were in the kitchen? And get me a ham and cheese sandwich with mayo."

As Logan retreated to the kitchen, Duke exited with the hat.

Duke scurried across the street to Levy's, the neighborhood clothing store. Upon entering the store he saw Irv Levy. "Irv, can you get a hat that looks exactly like this one?" The hat was greenish brown tweed with a brown band with a dark green feather.

"No problem, this is a common style, when do you want it?"

"In ten days, which will be next Thursday."

Duke knew that Thursdays were paydays and The Walk would be crowded with cops, fireman, construction workers, and a few downtown office workers.

"By the way Irv, I need a different size hat."

"What size?"

"Make it a size nine."

"What? You're buying a hat for an elephant?"

Duke exited the store chuckling, knowing that this sinister plot now had legs.

Duke entered The Widow's Walk with a large bag containing the sandwiches and the hat. He said, "Jimmy go in the back and get plates, I bought potato salad for us." While Logan was occupied in the kitchen, he placed the hat on the original hook.

While the two of them enjoyed their lunch, Duke's mind was ruminating about Logan's obsession of calling most men assholes. This designation by Logan was actually a term of endearment. If he didn't care for you, he would never call you an asshole. Actually, most guys considered it an honor to be designated an asshole by him. The strange thing about Logan was that curse words would never exit his mouth in the presence of women. Jimmy was old school in showing respect for the ladies.

That Thursday had finally arrived. Jimmy opened the bar and shortly after in came the Duke with tea and coffee. As they sipped their beverages, Duke stared intensely at Logan's head. "What the hell are you looking at?'.

"I don't know Jimmy, it looks like your head is smaller. Are you all right? You can tell me if there is something wrong."

"What the fuck are you talking about, you asshole? There is nothing wrong with me or my head."

These are the words Duke wanted to hear; the seed had been planted. Duke continued, "Jimmy, I left my gym bag in the car."

As Duke opened his car, he gently put the new hat into his gym bag before reentering the bar.

Duke told Logan, "It's payday, make sure there is enough ice." Begrudgingly, Logan retreated to the kitchen to get the ice and Duke switched the hats.

It was 11:30 a.m. and Duke left the bar telling Logan he was going to the gym. Duke returned at a couple of hours later and asked, "Everything OK, Jimmy?" as he zeroed in on Logan's head once more.

"Everything's fine asshole and stop staring at my head," said an enraged Logan.

Bobby Gilroy and two friends entered The Walk and sat at the end of the bar. Duke told them to wait fifteen minutes to ask Jimmy if there was something wrong with his head. The time had elapsed and Bobby Gilroy called Jimmy over.

"Want another drink, asshole?"

"I was wondering, what's wrong with your head? I don't know, but it looks like it shrunk."

Logan replied, as he pointed to Duke, "You know you're just like that asshole over there. There's nothing wrong with my head and I am healthy as ever."

Workers started to trickle into the bar. Duke intercepted them before they hit the bar stools and told them all of the cranial problems Logan had developed. During the remainder of Logan's shift, the voices of the arriving patrons quizzed Logan.

"Jimmy, do you have a fever or something your face is red and it looks like your head is effected?"

"Jimmy, did you come across an African tribe and they shrunk your head?"

"Jimmy, I don't think the doctors have a cure for that shrinking head of yours."

These head comments bombarded Logan from all directions. Logan's retort was a barrage of "You are an asshole!"

It was now closing in on six p.m. Jimmy was replenishing the ice and cleaning the bar for his relief. The Walk was packed with thirty guys and all of them had made reference to Logan's condition. Tom Flaherty was behind the bar and Jimmy was imbibing his first Manhattan, which was always his drink of choice. As he finished his drink, Tom asked him if he wanted another.

Logan said, "What do you think, asshole?"

"I guess that means yes", Tom replied. When Tom brought the second drink, he stared at Logan and asked if there was something wrong with his head.

"You too, asshole? I am fine. There is nothing, I mean nothing, wrong with my head!"

Logan was finishing his second drink which indicated he was about to exit The Walk. This farewell would be different however, as all the patrons heads slowly turned towards Logan.

Emphatically, Logan said, "What are you assholes looking at?" as he put on his long tweed coat. The stares intensified as he buttoned his coat and proclaimed, as he always did, "I go home to see my beloved."

The hat was removed from its hook and in a slow cadence he placed it on his supposed shrinking head. The hat continued on a methodical journey; first the forehead, then over his bloodshot eyes, and finally coming to rest at the tip of the nose, just short of his upper lip.

The silence gave way to uproarious laughter and a universal, "We told you your head was shrinking!"

Never removing the hat, Logan made his exit half-blinded, exclaiming that all present were assholes. He stopped before the door. There was Duke sitting on the last stool before the street. Logan approached him and gave the Duke the once over.

For five seconds there was no words spoken. Then Logan cracked a big grin and stated his usual, "You're an asshole."

Duke smiled. He gave Logan a hug and his hat back.

7

As Logan opened the door, he heard Duke say, "Jimmy, keep the other hat, you never know when your head will expand." They both cracked up.

Logan knew this would not be the end. There would be another time, another place, and another prank. It was unavoidable. But there would also be another steak dinner involving numerous alcoholic beverages which would cement the camaraderie between the two. That's how friends are, especially Bronx friends.

2
A Leap of Faith

Danny Walsh was just beginning his four block trek to The Widow's Walk. It was a soupy evening with a persistent, light rainfall that was going to make the night colder than it should be. The beginning of March in New York City was always a tug of war between winter and spring; tonight winter was winning.

A few hours before, he awoke with a raging hangover. Five and ten dollar bills were strewn all over him and the ability to remember a thing from Friday night to early Saturday morning was nonexistent. One thought persisted, however, he was in a card game and had an intense disagreement with a player thought to be cheating. This player eventually was forcefully removed from said game while screaming obscenities at him. This alcoholic blackout enabled him a slight remembrance of the occurrences, but a total blank on what his adversary looked like. It was as if he were a ghost.

Danny Walsh was five-foot-eleven, 190 pounds, with blue eyes and a pleasant face. He was a perfect fit for being one of The Widow's Walk bartenders. Danny entered the bar which signaled to the younger patrons that this night of controlled insanity was to begin, similar to the opening bell on Wall Street.

Logan was behind the bar and greeted him with the usual, "How's it going, asshole?" Logan continued, "Hmm, it looks like you had a tough Friday night chasing the girls," making reference to Walsh's bloodshot eyes. Walsh wished that were true, but at least he made money in the poker game. Danny saw the usual opening act for this night: Jigger McNally, Mike Paxton, Billy Woods, Paddy Allen, Chico Guinness and the only female, Maureen Drury.

The guys busted balls on each other with a few shots thrown at the bartender, which promoted a comedic camaraderie amongst all. Maureen was quiet, cute on the verge of evolving into a beautiful woman. She was always well dressed, definitely a few levels above her male compadres. Sitting next to the crew was Duke Callahan with an open chair waiting for Logan's arrival. All drinks had been delivered: a variety for Walsh's posse; the usual gin, soda, and splash of orange for Duke; and a standard Manhattan for Logan.

The phone rang. Danny gave the usual salutation, "Widow's Walk, can I help you?"

"Yeah," said the voice on the other end, "Is this Danny Walsh?" Walsh answered affirmatively. After a short silence, the voice spoke seriously and concise, "I am going to blow your fucking brains out tonight," after which the only sound was a dial tone.

All the after affects of the prior nights festivities intensified. He was paler than before, the headache was throbbing, the slight shaking of the body and hands took on volcanic proportions. In other words, Walsh was scared shitless and searching his mind for the description of the cheater from the game on Friday night. The cocktail blackout had reclaimed that part of his memory and would not give it up. Unfortunately, that was his situation. Danny was resigned to the fact that this could possibly be his last night on God's earth.

Walsh sought wisdom, sage advice, and empathy from the two gentlemen facing him. Yes, he would seek counsel from Duke and Logan.

"What do you think, Duke? Should I take tonight off?"

"If you run tonight Danny, then you will always run."

Walsh silently retorted, "What? What? This is advice?"

It was now Logan's turn, "Jimmy, you were a Bronx detective, what do you think I should do?"

Logan responded sharply, "You know, that's why you're an asshole. Do really think that someone would call you up and then kill you?"

"That's right Jimmy you know every homicidal maniac in the Bronx, why should I worry about a mere phone call?"

"Shut up, asshole. Make me another Manhattan."

And there it was, two voices of reasons not allaying Walsh's fears. Both men voicing their two unique philosophies, neither of which helped calm the inner turmoil besieging Danny's body and mind.

Duke stated that Logan and he were going to the Connolly's Steakhouse for dinner. Without verbally saying, Walsh mentally replied, "Oh, that's great Duke, that's really having my back in this life and death situation. I hope you and Logan have a great dinner while I am lying dead on the floor of your precious bar."

Duke and Logan left The Walk and the anxiety index for Walsh was increasing with each passing minute. He stared at every patron entering with a look that brought the response of "Did I do something wrong, Danny."

"No!" was Danny's response as he never divulged to the patrons the message of death he had receive. With this being the case, this cast of lunatics couldn't rationalize the deterioration of Danny's mental state. They just watched, as if it was a play, the physical and mental breakdown of their favorite bartender. No one would dare bust his balls causing an unusual silence throughout the bar. They saw him sweating a two-towel sweat because one would not be suffice to dry him off. He was shaking like a slightly overweight belly dancer. His pace behind the stick was amazing, the speed of a crazed antelope. Back and forth, back and forth, passing empty glasses that were screaming, "Can I have another?" The owner of said glasses dare not say a word. This was not their Danny Boy, it had to be some psychotic imposter.

The front door opened and in came a patron who had the misfortune of this being his very first time in The Widow's Walk. That's right a total stranger. He was wearing a black trench coat glistening with wintery raindrops. He was the same size and build as Walsh with blonde thinning hair. The stranger was standing by his presumed seat when Danny approached. Our hero didn't look at him; he glared at him without saying a word.

The gentleman opened his coat and beneath it he was wearing a fashionable sweater of the day. This particular garment had only two buttons fastening the sweater down by his waist. He reached down with his left hand to unfasten the two-button sweater. A move that was reminiscent of Jimmy Cagney retrieving a revolver in one of his gangster movies. Walsh leaped over the bar similar to an Olympic hurdler, grabbed the man by the throat, and started to strangle him. Walsh straddled his victim, strengthening his hold as the stranger's eyes were bulging out of head. All the patrons were standing in stunned silence as Walsh continued his assault.

The silence was broken by a determined declaration by Walsh, "So you're going to kill me, you fuck. I will show you, who will kill who."

At which time our brutalized stranger softly slurred these words, "All I wanted was a rum-and-coke." Danny released his grip, realizing that the man he was trying to reserve next Wednesdays nine a.m. funeral Mass for was not the stealth assassin in search of him. He gently assisted the young man to his stool while informing him that he will not be paying for any of his drinks this evening, coupled with a sincere apology from Walsh.

The crowd of twenty some-odd people were silent, but they were all thinking the same thing, "What the fuck just happened?" As our assault victim, who was later known to be one Jim Moore, a student at Fordham University, was attempting to readjust his breathing pattern. Walsh informed the crowd of what precipitated his violent outburst. All ears were concentrated on the tale from the prior night. It was as if Walsh was preaching from the pulpit at Saint Brendan's, instead of a homily from Father O'Boyle espousing love and peace. Walsh led his tiny congregation down a passage of controlled insanity and violence, emphasizing the violent aspect.

Danny raced into the kitchen and returned with a softball bat, so as to put and exclamation point on what awaits our unknown killer. His disturbed demeanor intensified as he quickly paced back and forth with bat in hand, only to stop periodically to serve a drink. No my friends, this was some serious shit, no joking, no ball busting. Some patrons were contemplating leaving, but were afraid to escape knowing that Walsh may whack them in the head before they made it to the door. In a strange way, they were all hostages, with the exception of Jim Moore who had just finished his third rum-and-coke, while his twenty-dollar bill remained unscathed. There they were observing Walsh's continuous back and forth pace quickening with bat still in hand. This man was a bonafide lunatic they thought, but never stated that fact.

There was another mysterious entrance into The Widow's Walk. Yes, yes, another man, but this one fit the part. Black hair, dark eyes, six-foot-one, 200 pounds, projecting a serious demeanor. It was as if he was the typical Hollywood gangster type cast. The black, trench coat reaffirmed, that this stranger was the culprit and he would be dealt with by way of a Louisville slugger! Walsh, with bat secreted behind him, and the stranger locked eyes. Not saying a word, the mystery man slowly turned his back while removing his coat. A muted gasp was heard while Walsh took his home run batting stance, like Mickey Mantle from the right side of the plate. The bat was posed to deliver a lethal blow. The man in black slowly turned and requested a Dewar's on the rocks. Danny gently flipped the Louisville to the floor with the grace of a slightly overweight ballerina, immediately making the drink.

Walsh's sweat engulfed his armpit and entire shirt, while his shaking was uncontrollable. He now had to ask Jigger what he wanted to drink even though he never drank anything but Vodka and orange for his whole life. It appeared that Walsh's demise would shortly arrive, but not by bullet. It would be suicide by insanity. Danny was past unraveled, as he now attained a stratospheric condition which gave way to a heart rate of 300 beats-per-minute and the internal combustibility that would produce the imminent stroke. Walsh was so convinced that he imagined his own obituary, "24-year old bartender succumbs to stroke. The parents request donations be made to American Heart Association instead of flowers." Walsh was contemplating introducing a butcher knife, to be a companion to his beloved softball bat.

Sean Duffy, five-foot-nine, cherubic face, brown eyes, and long, mousy brown hair entered the bar. Sean always portrayed unusual wit and physical presence. The physicality of his humor bordered on bazaar, but he was funny and all those present would throughly enjoy his antics. Sean continued his path down the bar noticing a macabre atmosphere had replaced the usual loud chatter and laughter.

He stood next to Jigger who whispered in Sean's ear, "There's been some crazy shit going on. Danny is totally out of his mind and it's getting worse. He is now in the kitchen looking for a butcher knife. About two hours ago, someone called him and told him that he was going to blow his fucking brains out. Since that call, he has been unraveling at a steady pace."

Sean's face turned ashen as Jigger noticed and said, "Don't tell me it was you?"

"Yeah, it was me. I thought it was like a joke. You know me."

"Some joke, you put him in two serious situations that could have resulted in 25-years-to-life in Attica prison."

Sean was now the one trembling. He knew not what awaited him as he approached the kitchen's entrance. Walsh slowly turned, while sharpening an eighteen-inch butcher knife, still with that crazed look in his eyes. "What's going on, Sean?"

Sean did not answer the question as he slowly approached Walsh. He fell to his knees and tightly grasped his hand. "It was me Danny, I'm the one who made the call, I'm so sorry."

A fit of homicidal insanity entered Walsh's already demented mind. The situation took a radical change as he looked down at Sean with a devilish grin. The fear Walsh felt was gone as if he had unloaded his sins in the confessional booth. He was now violence free. Yes, Sean's words had cleansed him and he felt the old Danny Boy coming back.

"Sean, how can I be mad at you? Why didn't you call back and say it was a goof?"

"I don't know, I just thought you would think it was a joke. You know how weird my sense of humor can be."

"Some joke. Guess what? The only one who will be pissed at you is Duke. See that guy at the end of the bar? He is on his fifth rum-and-coke and his twenty-dollar bill has yet to been touched. Yeah, he's the guy I almost strangled to death."

Sean and Danny looked at each other and started laughing uncontrollably. That, my friends, is Bronx humor.

DANNY HOFER

3
Mickey O

It was a beautiful morning on the last Friday of April 1970 and The Widow's Walk was unusually crowded. There were two foursomes of golfers ready to depart for the links of Van Cortlandt Park, the designated country club of the Bronx. Positioned at the far end of the bar was Mickey O'Grady, the neighborhood bookie, guarding his turf which included the bar's payphone. To Mickey O's left, was Buster Reilly's construction crew. Buster and his men were studying their racing forms with the intensity of a group of prelaw students.

Thursday was payday, and Buster had the boys start to imbibe at eight a.m. and drink all day, instead of working. At three-thirty they were released, as if being paroled from an alcoholic penitentiary with Buster as the self appointed warden.

His credo was simple, "You will not work today, but you will drink until quitting time. That's the way it will be."

However, this week they changed days. The boys worked on Thursday and Buster used Friday as a scheduled racetrack day. Buster loved Belmont Racetrack and its picnic area. This Friday, he had the men fill the giant cooler that was kept in the steamfitter shanty, with three cases of beer. He sent Bobby Gilroy next door to Frank's Deli to pick up the preordered six-foot long hero.

There was only one thing left to do, and that one thing was to bet. Buster and his gang had a perfect arrangement with Mickey O. They would settled up with Mickey on the next payday, win or lose. Buster and his crew continued handicapping until 10:30. Then, without being prodded, they formed a line by Mickey O and gave him all their individual bets. They all figured betting this way allowed them to not bet actual US tender at the track.

That was the method to this group's madness. However, there was one problem to this logic. The more they drank at the track, the more they would soften their self discipline and start to reach in their pockets to unload their cash at the betting windows. This was the quintessential double-edge sword. No matter which way it swung, it would most likely render negative results for the boys.

Duke Callahan was nursing his second cup of coffee as he observed the construction wagering in the corner. He was interrupted by the two foursomes who were ready to depart. They requested that Duke fill up four thermoses with Bloody Marys. Duke obliged, after which he bid adieu to the soon to be buzzed up golfers. He returned to his coffee and watched Mickey O in action. Duke was always impressed by Mickey's demeanor.

Duke knew Mickey O had personality, along with a math prowess that gave him the ability to remember bets if he was unable to write them down on paper. He often wondered, if his friend had gone to the right side of the tracks, how successful would he have been. He could have envisioned Mickey O pursing academics and successfully entering the business world, but he knew him too well.

They were both the same age and grew up as close friends. He remembered when they were both in fifth grade and Mickey's mother had died after being struck by a bus. The ten-year-old Mickey was scarred for life after the tragedy and his self-imposed guilt never subsided. A guilt that would never leave him because to this day, it was he who had suddenly darted out into the street, to retrieve his Spaldeen ball. That action resulted in his mothers instinct to protect her child. It was that lifesaving motion that propelled his mother towards the bus collision; a collision that would render no possible chance of survival.

Mickey's mental turmoil was evident when he would over imbibe with the Duke. Duke would see his eyes moisten as a deluge of hurt would stream down his face.

He would place his hand gently on Mickey's shoulder and softly tell his friend that it was time to forgive himself. He would continue that his sainted mother, Eileen, in her soft County Kerry brogue would chastise him for the self-imposed hell. She would tell you that there is nothing to forgive and note it was just a horrible chain of events. Finally, she would tell you of the depth of her love for you and how it would be a joyous day when you and she would reunite in heaven.

Duke knew because of this event that Mickey, at age ten and the oldest of four, had to work to help his father financially.

This was when the great man, Big Tim Tobin, came to the rescue. Big Tim became the local bookie as soon as World War II was over. Tim and all the young men in the neighborhood were home in 1946. The economy was healthy and the men were working various blue collar jobs. Jobs that availed of them extra money which they could spend on social pleasures. One of these pleasures was gambling.

Tim was quite the gambler himself. When there was a lull in combat he would run a crap game in the back of a two-and-a-half-ton troop transport, that was conveniently out of sight of the military police. Tim did quite well for himself. So well, that his ruck sack was stuffed with US currency in place of a sleeping bag. He gave his sleeping bag to a buddy to carry for a five-dollar weekly payment. Tim and his pal made it through the war unscathed. On the troop ship bound for New York, Tim had his small fortune packed safely in a duffle bag.

Tim Tobin knew the O'Grady family because he lived in the same Webster Avenue tenement. He was always cordial to the O'Gradys when passing in the hallways. They would have short chit-chat conversations, which were the extent of their socializing. It would change that day in May 1947, the day of the horrific accident and the death of Mrs. O'Grady. Tim heard of the incident while setting up shop at Donnelly's Pub. Upon hearing the news, he made the sign of the cross and said a heartfelt prayer for Eileen O'Grady and family.

Two weeks after the funeral, the whole clan were home preparing for dinner and heard the knock on the door. Mickey opened the door and there he was, the man himself, Tim Tobin. Mickey saw a man who measured six foot four, broad shoulders, with a harden face that almost diminished the twinkle in his blue eyes. Mickey called out to his dad that Mr. Tobin was at the door. Pat O'Grady came to the door and while shaking Tim's hand had a queried look on his face. Why was Big Tim in front of him? Tim, once again, extended his condolences on the passing of Eileen.

Tim in a low soft tone said, "Pat, I'm a single man and probably will be one for life. I'll never experience the burdens of fatherhood and the awesome responsibility of raising a family. I'll never know the rigors put on parents financially while constantly keeping the children on the strait and narrow. Those obligations are intensified when one of the parents passes on. Pat, you are a man I have great respect for. You're a righteous man with tremendous pride and rightfully so."

Tim went into his coat pocket and retrieved an envelope. As he passed the envelop to Pat, Tim continued, "Take this. It is not a Franciscan food-line charity for the bowery bums. It is however, a gift to a man I hold in great esteem. You're a man I could never emulate. Please Pat, take this. It will help pay for your recent unexpected expenses."

Pat opened the envelope and it contained thirty twenty-dollar bills which at that time was a whole lot of money. Pat was silent for ten seconds pondering two scenarios. One would be a gracious return of the money stating, "We'll manage by our selves, thank you." The other was to graciously accept. Pat turned his head and peered at his four little ones making busy in the kitchen. Pat knew this money would greatly help lessen the burdens of purchasing food and clothing. Pat slowly turned and faced Tim, head half way bowed in embarrassment, and said, "Thank you, Tim, I'll accept your gift."

Tim placed his big, right paw on Pat's left shoulder. Speaking a low tone so that only he could hear, Tim said, "Pat, I'll never experience the burdensome task of a single parent raising four children. You should be lionized and heralded for your fine example of fatherhood. This is a noble effort needed to establish the foundation of our great country. Pat, I love this country and by helping you and your family, I am doing my small part to ensure the legacy of the United States of America. It should be me thanking you for what you are doing, not you thanking me."

The two men did a six-inch stare for a few seconds and both smiled simultaneously.

Pat, with moistened eyes said, "Tim, you're a good man."

Tim cracked a devilish grin, "I don't know about that Pat, maybe I am one half of a good man. Now, my friend, I have to go to Donnelly's to open up shop."

Both firmly shook hands and off Big Tim went.

Two days later, Tim was coming down the stairs as Mickey was exiting his apartment.

"Hello, Mr. Tobin."

"Hello, Mickey Boy and how are you on this fine day?"

"OK, but I am having a hard time finding a job because of my age. I'm ten and can't get working papers and no one in the neighborhood will hire me."

Tim halted their exit from the building as he turned towards Mickey and said, "Would you like to work for me on Saturdays? I would only need you once a day and I'll give you $10 for your effort."

Mickey was a street wise kid and he knew of Big Tim's occupation. Respectfully, he said, "Mr. Tobin"

"Call me Tim!"

"Tim, I don't think my father would like this type of work."

"Lad, we do not want to worry your father. Lord knows he has enough on his plate. Let's say we'll create a small white lie. I have another apartment on Webster Avenue. The apartment is used once in a while for business, but it's a God awful mess and needs tending to. Tell your father you have to show up every Saturday at noon to clean the place. OK?"

Mickey gave a quizzical affirmative nod.

"If your father agrees, knock on my door, apartment 5G, at ten a.m. this Saturday."

Tim exited the building and Mickey went back to his apartment to talk to his father. His father was in the kitchen having a cup of tea when Mickey approached him with Tim's proposition. After some cajoling, Pat hesitantly agreed.

"Thanks, daddy, he is going to pay me $10 that I will give it all to you."

Pat proudly smiled at his son, although it appeared to have the makings of a mysterious caper. "Son, any man that puts in a day's work must be rewarded, you give me five and you keep five."

The next Saturday, Big Tim told Mickey to go to the rear door of Donnelly's at noon. When Mickey arrived, he was given a shopping bag filled with racing forms and all the horse bets taken from Donnelly's. Mickey had to hustle to Morrison's Bar where phone man, Tom Clark, was outside ready to take the shopping bag. Clark, then entered Morrison's to take horse and sports bets from the customers.

This routine continued throughout grammar school and high school for Mickey. After graduation from high school, Mickey turned eighteen and volunteered for the service. He served his military time stationed on the DMZ in Korea. When he was discharged in 1957, he had fully matured physically and mentally.

Mickey arrived home on a Saturday morning in early autumn. His father greeted him with an affectionate bear hug, along with his two younger brothers and his sister grasping joyously at his uniform and hat. They all celebrated that evening with a steak dinner at Connelly's. Mickey politely answered all the question about his time in Korea, while his siblings gazed starry-eyed as he spoke.

His father's chest exploded with pride as he was engulfed by his son's presence. He realized his job was done for the elder.

He saw a striking handsome, personable young man ready to take on the world. No more fatherly lessons needed, only the periodic advice when asked. Pat smiled and gave himself a silent "at-a-boy" on a job well done.

He suddenly stopped his self appraisal and mentally scolded himself, "Why the hell am I taking credit? How could I be so self indulged?" He knew Eileen was the main influence. She instilled in Mickey the rights and wrongs of life. She formed that sturdy backbone which made him stick to his principles, no matter how difficult it may be. Pat realized that it was her loving, kind demeanor which infected all persons she came in contact with, and that influenced Mickey the most. Eileen created a small nook in Mickey's heart dedicated to the niceties of life: love, compassion, kindness to all, and forgiveness, for without it who will forgive you. Generosity, as much as you can tolerate, because you never know when you could be on the last rung of the ladder of life. Virtues as these, many believed, can't evolve in a working, poor culture. Wrong! They constantly occurred in that environment, but they didn't get the hoopla of the generosity of a Carnegie or a Rockefeller. These virtues seemingly went unnoticed, but not by those who were on the receiving end.

Pat's thoughts drifted back to the present and there he saw his family smiling and happy. He turned towards Mickey and saw an intense stare. Mickey's eyes were focused on his father the entire time. He knew what was behind his father's elongated silence. Pat was thinking of Eileen. The noise of the steakhouse was muted as the two men half smiled at each other. Pat placed his right hand on Mickey's neck and felt its rigidity because he knew there was turmoil within his son and he knew the reason why.

Pat whispered, "Mickey Boy, you're my son and I know you, oh so well. Son, you have to forgive yourself and erase this guilt from your mind."

Mickey softly responded, "Pop, I am always trying. But when we have a joyous occasion as this with the whole family, that horrific incident with mom enters my being as if it was a monster sent from the depths of hell. It just happens and I can't control it."

Pat brought Mickey's face towards his and gently stroked his son's head. As they connected, the few tears from their moistened eyes were dried by each others cheeks.

With the prior nights festivities over, the family woke up the next morning and attended Mass at Saint Brendan's. Mickey excused himself after breakfast and went to Donnelly's Pub to see Duke and the boys.

They consumed a few drinks after which Mickey went to the other end of the bar and saw Big Tim manning the pay phone. When their eyes met, Big Tim slowly extended his six-foot-four frame and joyously embraced Mickey.

"Welcome home, boyo, you've done your country proud."

After a few exchanged pleasantries, Tim said, "I know it's a bit soon, Mickey, but what are your future plans? Do you have any inclinations of what might please you?"

"Tim, I want to work for you."

"Mickey, you're such a bright lad. Go to college, graduate, and go knock the shit out of Wall Street."

"Tim, it's not for me. They're a different sort. They're elitist snobs."

"Son, they have all the wealth and the accompanying trinkets: beautiful homes, expensive cars, and private schools that their spoiled kids attend."

"Tim, that's all they have, they are purely materialistic beings. Their plastic demeanor with all the patting on the back, insincere smiles, and cut throat attitude is what I personally despise. No Tim, it's not for me. I would be punching out those scumbags by the numbers."

Tim with a confused smile said, "All right, son, work for me you will. I'll have you taking sports bets from that apartment you were cleaning for all those years. Tom Clark is pulling the pin and off to Florida next month. He'll introduce you to all the bettors in Morrison's. Mickey, it's not as easy as it seems. You have to contend with people not paying, possible arrest, carrying a lot of cash which can make you a mark for some bad guys. There is no retirement pension or social security.

"You can't be like the bettors. You have to abstain, only participate in the gamble when you have the best of it. By avoiding these negatives, you will be able to stash enough cash for your later years."

Mickey listened intently to Tim and said, "You know why I already know the pitfalls, Tim? Because I watched you throughout

29

my teen years. You were successful because of your talents and discipline. I have seen that and I want to be part of it."

Tim smiled and softly cuffed Mickey on the chin. He extended his big Irish mitt and shook Mickey's hand saying. "We've got a deal."

Mickey asked Tim if he could rent the apartment where he was going to take the action. Tim agreed and told Mickey to pay $30 which was only half the rent.

"Why half, Tim?"

"Mickey, consider it a monthly bonus for a job well done."

Mickey left Tim beaming, but now he had to let his father know he would be getting his own apartment.

Arriving home he let Pat know of his intentions. He also made up a fictitious job at a restaurant bar and grill where Mickey would be the full-time, night bartender. He told Pat that he would take the New York Central Railroad to Mount Kisco and then either take a cab or have one of the waiters pick him up.

Pat was suspiciously happy for his son. Mickey knew his father didn't have a car and with three children in high school didn't have the time to take a train to Mount Kisco.

"Dad, after I get established, I will buy a used car which will make the commute much easier."

Pat queried, "How the hell can you afford the rent in the Regency Arms?"

"Pop, I am going to split the rent with Duke Callahan."

Pat half smiled telling Mickey, "I knew this day would come when my boy would sprout his wings and fly away to chase his dreams. I am going to miss you, Michael, but you will always have a place to come home to if things don't work out."

Two days later, Duke Callahan, Neil Conlin, and Tom Gilroy came to the O'Grady apartment to help with Mickey's move. When the move was completed, Mickey extended his hand to his father.

Suddenly, Pat engulfed his son in a tight embrace and whispered, "Remember the legacy your mother taught. Live by it and you will always be in the right. Remember son, I will always love you no matter what." Pat, while slowly releasing his grasp gently kissed his son on the cheek.

It was done. Mickey was free. The freedom wasn't an easy freedom, for it wasn't freedom from bondage. It was negative in nature, for there was no longer that embracing security blanket that emanated from one's family. Yes, he was now to go it alone. It was exhilarating and at the same time nauseously depressing. Sure, externally, he still had family and friends, but in those moments of solitude and loneliness, he had only his inner being that would keep him company.

He immediately went to work taking numbers and horses from the apartment. Mickey took the sports action from Morrison's Bar from six to eight p.m. weekly. He would take off Tuesday because the New York tracks were closed. Johnny Ryan manned the phones for numbers and sports. Johnny was a retired sanitation worker. He would take all the action from Donnelly's and Morrison's while Big Tim and Mickey were off.

On those days, they both tightened the bond between each other. They met Tuesday at the Greenleaf and had pre-dinner drinks. It was always the Greenleaf because the owner, Billy O'Hara, was a great guy and a good friend. Billy directed all the betting action from his bar to Big Tim which also didn't hurt. Big Tim would buy a few rounds for the patrons and with his good nature would always allowed to have his balls busted by his fellow blue-collar boozers. They never saw Tim as a rich guy who put himself above them; they saw him as the noble bookmaker with a big heart. Big Tim had their loyalty and above all their betting action.

These Tuesdays, between four and six p.m., the drinking pace increased along with the one-line ball busting.

A voice from the crowd shouted, "Hey, Tim, what are you gonna do with all that money and who you gonna leave it too?"

Tim replied, "Don't know who I'll leave it to, but it won't be you, asshole."

The laughter increased along with the drinking pace. O'Hara smiled, he knew that Tuesday afternoon was the most profitable time from Monday to Thursday.

Then another quip from the bar, "Hey Tim, when you gonna get rid of that piece of shit you're driving and get a new Cadillac? Yeah, a car that reflects your status, oh my great, high, exalted bookie-ness."

More laughter while Tim snapped back, "Hey dipshit, you don't have two nickels to rub together and you're insulting my, lets say dated, vehicle. After all it's a classic."

Yet another patron yelled, "Yeah, it's a classic, like my brand new asshole after my hemorrhoid operation."

Laughter erupted an octave higher.

Tim said to Sean the bartender, "Give those two wise asses a drink. No, Sean, wait why should those two assholes be special; buy the whole bar."

Six p.m. arrived and Tim elbowed Mickey saying, "Let's get something to eat."

They exited the Greenleaf after leaving Sean a hefty tip. This routine never changed for all the years they would be together. These weekly feasts started with martinis and appetizers, followed by a Porter House steak and all the trimmings with an expensive bottle of wine. The dinners ended with dessert and coffee plus a combo of scotch and Drambuie, known as a Rusty Nail. These occasions lasted about two hours. This was when Mickey's ears perked as he was engrossed by every word Tim uttered. He always listened intently to Tim because he was a "deez demz and doz" street philosopher, who knew the pros and cons of all life's endeavors. Why? Because he lived every day as though it was his last. Big Tim had to, because there was no security net and if he fucked up, there was only one person to blame. It was him. He experienced the niceties and goodness of life along with its darkened step-brother, evil. Tim, after a short conversation with any individual, could determine if the person was solid or full of shit. Mickey appreciated his wisdom and wanted to consume all that informative guidance Tim voiced. Mickey desired to be a young Tim and these weekly tutorials laid the foundation.

In 1965, Big Tim brought Mickey in as a partner and they split everything fifty-fifty, no contract needed. Tim was not part of the operation as Mickey ran the whole show for his fifty percent. Mickey hired Johnny Ryan to be the full-time man at Donnelly's and two other guys split the work at Morrison's. Mickey still answered the phones at the apartment and calculated the work for the week showing the wins and losses. The action showed Big Tim and Mickey winning for the week most of the time. During the last five years, his father knew Mickey was not in the restaurant business. He heard the neighborhood rumors, but they never fazed him. Pat knew his son was a decent man, whose foundation was built on principled character. He knew his son was generous and treated all with respect and revered the neighborhood's moral dignity.

Mickey saw his brothers and sister arrive safely into adulthood. They all went to college and landed solid occupations. One brother to Wall Street, one to the NYPD, and his darling, baby sister became a Kindergarten teacher in the NYC school system.

The darkest day of sixties was December 27, 1966 when Mickey lost his beloved father. The occurrence catapulted him into a depression for the remainder of the winter. He was never one-hundred-percent after his father's demise, just as his mother's put a hurt in his heart that would never heal.

The day of Pat's passing and the following week, Tim took all the action and let Mickey be. He knew the young man was hurting and that time alone could diminish the pain, but never eliminate it. Ten days later, Mickey returned and resumed his daily regimen. He took the action from the apartment during the day.

Tuesday night still brightened his heart; strangely he was still learning from Big Tim. He cherished their dinners because Tim was now narrowing the gap between here and the Lord. Tim was just about sixty and had made it a point to live life furiously and it showed. Physically, he was dangerously overweight, had epic high blood pressure, was pre-diabetic along with facial features that portrayed the ravages of time. Mentally, though, he had the mind of a senior at the Bronx High School of Science. His humor never diminished and his attachment to his protege became an unbreakable bond. Tim had only Mickey as his family. The business ran smoothly throughout the sixties and in 1969, the two partners added another bar, The Widow's Walk, which was owned by Duke Callahan, Mickey's best friend.

It was May 16, 1969 when Mickey O received a call from The Widow's Walk. Bartender Moose Morano was on the phone and told him something terrible happened to Big Tim.

"Big Tim was at the bar doing his usual schtick, when he fell off the bar stool and onto the floor. Luckily, Paddy Allen, who had

35

been a medic in Vietnam, got to Tim in a flash and revived him with CPR.

"He was semi-conscious when the ambulance arrived and took him to Montefiore emergency. That's all I know,"

Mickey ran out onto Webster Avenue, hailed a cab, and made haste to Montefiore Hospital. The cabby got to the emergency entrance in a matter of minutes and Mickey ran into the entrance. He saw the attendants usher Big Tim into one of the many curtained areas used to treat patients. Mickey noticed two doctors, barely thirty years of age, and a young nurse rush to Big Tim. They were behind the curtain for some time, barking out medical terminology, that was undecipherable to the average person. Mickey heard noise and commotion and after forty-five minutes a strange calm emanated. A whispered speak was heard that could only be picked up by some type of sonar.

The hush tones ended as the curtain was opened. Mickey saw the medical staff, but he couldn't see Big Tim because they blocked his view. He watched the attendants and a nurse speed Tim's gurney out the rear area. Mickey tried to follow, but was stopped by a security guard, who directed him to one of the attending doctors.

"How's he doing?" Mickey queried.

Dr. Anthony Gurry inquired if he was family.

"Yes, doctor, I'm his nephew and was informed about what happened about an hour ago."

The doctor responded, "Seeing you are family, I can inform you that your uncle suffered a massive heart attack and still alive because of the CPR rendered at the scene. Coupled with the fact that he is so powerfully built, he had the stamina to hang in there."

Mickey, with a wry smile, said. "Yes, that's my uncle Tim, strong as an ox and stubborn as a mule."

The doctor smiled and continued speaking in a serious manner, "Mr. --"

"O'Grady."

"Well, Mr. O'Grady, your uncle, I'm afraid may have suffered irreparable damage to his heart. We are going to do all the tests necessary to determine how much damage. For now, you should go home. Your uncle will be undergoing procedures until tomorrow. Please, give me your phone number, in case I have to get in touch with you."

Mickey didn't want to give the doctor the apartment phone number, instead he gave him Duke Callahan's number. Duke would get in touch with him if necessary.

He turned from the doctor and exited the hospital onto the street. Once on the pavement, a sickening, morose feeling overwhelmed him. He started to shake uncontrollably as tears streamed rapidly down his cheeks. He thought that Big Tim would be with him forever. Big Tim was the last mooring Mickey could anchor to. He lost his mom and dad, but he never thought he would lose Big Tim.

Tim, in a strange way, sheltered him from the everyday evil and good that the passing of time brought. His everyday common sense tutorials directed how Mickey would live his life. The emptiness intensified as he realized that there was a possibility of never experiencing Tim's outlandish demeanor and humor that had endeared him to all who knew him. Mickey experienced the uncertainty, the loneliness, and the feeling of being abandoned, as if he were a five year old trekking off to his first day of kindergarten.

He took the long walk back to the neighborhood so he could clear his head. He stopped at The Widow's Walk to have a drink and talk to Duke Callahan. Mickey told Duke that the doctor had his phone number and would call if there was any emergency. After fifteen minutes of chit chat, he left Duke and went home.

Tomorrow would be an emotionally filled day. Mickey's sleep that night was anything but. He tossed and turned until the wee dawn hours. At five his exhaustion took over as he fell into a deep sleep for three hours. Eight a.m. arrived. Mickey groggily threw off his covers, showered, and got dressed. He gulped down a cup of instant Maxwell House along with two slices of burnt toast slathered with Kerry Gold Irish butter.

As Mickey locked the door behind him, the sickening feeling from the previous night overtook him once again. It diminished somewhat as the morning sun warmed him while he ventured up Bainbridge Avenue on his way to the hospital.

He inquired at the front desk what room Tim was in. The young woman behind the desk directed him to Room 516 located in the Intensive Care Unit.

Mickey arrived at the fifth floor and was told he could only stay thirty minutes, leave for four hours and then come back for another short visit. Before going to see Tim, he was able to speak to the doctor on duty, who just happened to be Dr. Gurry.

"Hello, Mr. O'Grady, unfortunately my first diagnosis was correct. Your uncle had a heart attack and on a scale of one to ten, it was a nine. The only reason it wasn't a ten is because a ten is the point of no return. He is resting peacefully and is not in any pain, so you can visit. I'll extend your visit to one hour because last night I saw the loving concern for your uncle. I think the extended visit might brighten his spirit. I want you to realize, Mr. O'Grady, the man you will visit now is not the man you knew one week ago."

Mickey turned and quietly tip toed into the room which was bright with sun rays dancing from wall to wall. Mickey was afraid. He wanted to leave, but realized if the situation was reversed Big Tim would never leave. Tim would embrace the moment because it was his boy, Mickey, whom he would never abandon. Mickey, slowly approached Tim's bed and what he saw, startled him. There was Tim, half asleep, his face ashen grey as were his eyes. The eyes that danced with joy and always portrayed his devilish personality. Also, absent was the dimpled smile and the cherry lips, now chalk white.

Mickey whispered, "Tim it's me."

As Tim slowly widened his eyes, he saw him and gently grabbed his hand.

"There's my Mickey Boy,"

"Tim, as soon as I heard last night, I came here, but they wouldn't let me see you. I'm here now and I'll stay til they throw me out, like they do in Morrison's when I've had too much to drink."

Tim sported a diminished grin. He raised his big Irish mitt and motioned for Mickey to come closer. Mickey obliged and their faces were six inches apart. Big Tim was about to issue his final edict.

Tim began emotionless and in a monosyllabic cadence, "From the first day I met you, I knew you were someone special. You were past smart, you were intelligent and that's a big difference. Smart guys can be wise asses and think they are sharper than they actually are. They don't have the intelligence quotient you possess and that's big. You're able to realize you have to improve, or try to, every day. You don't rest on your laurels. You understand the average person and would never hurl wise cracking, condescending remarks to our customers. Like a priest, you keep the transactions between our office and the bettors secret. The wiseass violates all these rules of behavior."

Tim motioned Mickey to get his pants hanging in the closet. Obediently, he retrieved the pants while Tim told him to remove his keys from the right pocket. Mickey was bewildered.

"You see that key, take it off the chain. Remember, about five years ago, I presented you with an official bank card that had my signature on it. I wanted you to sign underneath my signature."

Mickey didn't recall.

"Well, this is the key to my safe deposit box. I made an arrangement with the bank official so that you would have access to the box. I gave them all your pertinent information which enables you to retrieve what ever you need."

Tim whispered the combination to his personal safe. Tim told Mickey to get two pieces of paper and write the numbers down and put them in his right and left pants pockets. Tim pointed to his apartment key and told him to take it along with the security box key.

"Those keys will insure that you have financial security. The apartment safe contains a large bag of diamonds and numerous gold coins preserved in mint condition. Remove them and get your own security box at another bank. My security box is the largest the bank had available. The box is crammed full of hundred-dollar bills."

"Tim why are you doing this? In two weeks time, we will be at the Greenleaf getting our balls busted and buying rounds of drinks. Then, it will be off to Connolly's Steakhouse, talking business, laughing, eating and drinking like we do every Tuesday."

An elongated silence was broken by Tim's ever weakening voice, "I am not leaving here."

Mickey barked, "Don't say that. You will be all right. I need you, Tim." Mickey's eyes started to well over and before the tears flowed, Tim softly touched Mickey's cheek and began his final philosophical tutorial.

"I am so afraid now, more afraid than I was in World War II. I don't know what's ahead. I just don't want to be a solitary spirit, alone for eternity. It cost me greatly. I never had a woman to be my life mate. Sure, I had my share of women, they came and went like the passage of time. Never, to be for me, was the nightly peck on the cheek, how was your day lovey? Never, would I come home periodically with a dozen roses saying, come on darlin', you work so hard, let's dress up and go to whatever restaurant you desire. Never would I, after saying those words see the eyes of a person who truly loved me and me only. Never would I, be able to see children of mine transition from birth to adulthood. I would never be able to experience all their various accomplishments along the way. I'll never feel that fatherly pride one gets when a child exceeds in their endeavorers.

"No, Mickey Boy, I am a loner. Sure, when I was a younger man, the freedom and the fact that I could do whatever I wanted with no restrictions was exhilarating. Now as I lie here, I feel so inadequate because I never participated in the dance of life, I was always a bystander. There was a time, however, when life availed me the opportunity to experience a departure from my self-exiled solitude. It began when we first met and shook hands. Our relationship started as being close friends, then it became sort of a

42

big brother, but I can never say, father, because you had the best. You availed me to have a smidgen of being able to truly care for another. Thank you, boy."

Mickey was stunned. He never saw this side of Big Tim. The complexities and emotions were never evident in their daily interactions.

"Come on, Tim hang in there. No one has more fight than you."

Tim grasped Mickey's hand, so tight it was uncomfortable, but he didn't care.

Tim spoke again, just above a soft whisper, "I am past the priest. I haven't confessed since eighth grade in Saint Brendan's, so I would be a hypocrite if I did so now. Therefore, I ask you this, have I been good to others? Did I ever welch on a handshake? I only hope that my occupation was not responsible for destroying a person's life."

His grip lessened. "I know I was cross with you once in a while, but remember, it was always a teaching moment. I developed a love for you as if you were my son. I just hope, in the depth of your heart, you might have considered me a surrogate father since the passing of your dad."

Tim's grasp loosened and it was now Mickey's hand holding Tim's tightly.

"As I said before, what am I going to do without you? Tim, as far as questioning your own morality, well, it was never in question. You're as moral as they come. It's not the Sunday Masses

43

and confessions that makes a man of virtue. Look at all those lace curtain Irish going to Mass, bowing their heads so piously, pounding their chests in supposed contrition and devotion. Those types leave the pew, exit the church, and jump at the first opportunity to screw over one of their associates with a knife stabbing in the back. Their handshakes are worthless. I'd rather cut my hand off than make a deal with the devil on earth. Jesus Christ, Tim, compared to the so called moral country club elite, you should be canonized.

"From day one, you have had a positive affect on my life. You said, if someone doesn't pay you, take it on the chin because you're the one who took the bet. I watched what you did for working guys who got in a little too deep. You saw the financial strain of a weekly effort to pay off a debt. You knew he had a family of small children. Unknown to all, you would forgive that debt, with a firm warning that this would never happen again. That person would never be able to bet with you again.

"No one in the neighborhood knew about the many times you helped a family in need. You would give them an envelope filled with cash expecting nothing back except a simple thank you. Tim, that's Godliness.

"I heard the big guy upstairs likes your act. He repeatedly tells St. Peter there's Big Tim, at it again. You know, he might not be perfect, but I do love it when he does My work on earth."

Tim was weakening, but still able to foster a smile as he whispered, "Mickey, you're some Irish storyteller. That tale lifted

44

my heart, but do you really think I did enough to be able to see the Gates of Heaven."

"Tim, you did more than your share to get into the winner's circle."

Tim chuckled which caused him to cough. He started to gasp for air and it seemed to take the fight out of him. Mickey squeezed Tim's hand as hard as he could, but Tim was losing his fight with death.

"Mickey stay with me. I know I will be just fine as I pass over. Mickey, Mickey, don't leave me." Those were Big Tim's last words. Mickey ran out of the room to summon the medical personnel, but it was too late, Big Tim was gone.

Mickey left the hospital physically and mentally drained. He walked the streets aimlessly, never hinting at a destination. Eventually, he found himself on Jerome Avenue and the noise of the el train brought him back to reality.

He knew where he had to go. It was the place where all families dreaded: Mike Doherty's Funeral Home. Mike Doherty greeted Mickey. Before he could inquire, Mickey blurted out, "Big Tim Tobin is dead and I will take care of all the expenses. Mike, I would like to have a one night wake and the funeral Mass the next day said by the beloved Father O'Boyle."

The day of the wake came, Mickey dressed up in his only suit, shined his shoes and made haste to Doherty's. The wake proved that the Church would be packed for the funeral Mass, and that it was. Mickey walked directly behind the casket followed by all of Tim's cronies and customers. They were the only family he had. There they were: construction men in their work clothes, bartenders, Wall Street guys, cops, firemen, and other book makers. It was a menagerie of all stars. If ever a funeral Mass was unique, this one was one for the books.

Father O'Boyle was Bronx raised. His flock was the working poor. He loved them and they in turn adored him because he was one of them. His sermon was sprinkled with various escapades about Tim, who he was, and how he treated people.

Even though it wasn't publicized, Father O'Boyle was well aware of Tim's generosity. He referred to a night when Tim knocked on the Rectory door and asked to see him. Tim found out that funds were needed for uniforms, equipment, and league fees for the parish basketball team. Big Tim handed me an envelope with $500. He said with a chuckle, "Let's say it's a down payment for me to slip through the pearly gates."

Father O'Boyle continued his sermon. "On balmy summer nights, I would stroll the neighborhood and converse with parishioners. My last stop was always Morrison's Bar where I would have a Cutty Sark on the rocks nightcap. Tim would always say, 'This man's money is no good.' He always approached me with his infectious smile. During our conversation, he would inquire if some one or some family fell on hard times. 'Please let me know Father. You're going to be my angel spy. I want to do some good, but I don't want any one to know it was me.'"

Father O'Boyle took a long pause after praising Big Tim.

"I know many of you are puzzled by the mystery of faith. You may feel that Mass and Confession can't be the only indicators of whether you are truly a Christian. You all know there is more to it. You are right to assume that participating in Mass, Confession, Holy Days of Obligation and adhering to the sacraments are the only the parameters of Catholicism. To be a true follower of Christ, you must be a Christian.

"Many of you are saying sarcastically, 'Wow, Father! Like we didn't know that.' Well, my dear friends, many Catholics may know that, but they don't practice the Christian spirit throughout their lives. They feel that their commitments to the obligations of Catholicism is enough and that they did their fair share and thus, will enjoy eternity with Our Savior.

"I like to call Tim an unusual and complex Catholic. He was proud to be Catholic, but didn't adhere to any of the dictates of our religion. I know that sounds contradictory and some would think immoral, but that's how Tim lived his life. Tim's saving grace was that he aggressively sought out opportunities to practice the true mandates of Christianity. His acts of kindness and charity abounded, but he kept these acts to himself. One would never hear Tim crow and say, I did this or I did that. A firm handshake and thank you was sufficient. What he did for an individual or family was a forgotten memory, never to be brought up again.

"Others practice kindness, but use it as a bargaining chip. They remind people that in their time of need, you helped them out and you expect some sort of return in the future. That, my friends,

47

is not what Jesus preached. It's an act of charity on the outside, but inside its a vacuous self-serving act that was premeditated from the start.

"In closing, we all know that Tim had his negatives and positives, but don't we all. I know this. When Big Tim closed his eyes for the last time on earth, he reopened them and was engulfed by the angels who escorted him to the throne. Our Lord welcomed him with a quizzical smile and a wink. The Lord said, 'You know my favorite angels are the ones I refer to as the mischievous bunch. I know you're closed lip, don't tell the other angels. Tim, that's where you are going, to the mischievous bunch. I will use you once in a while to go to earth to help people desperate and in need. After all, that's what you did during your time on earth.' Our Lord stood up and walked toward Tim. He saw Tim's tears as he embraced him. He gently wiped the tears away, saying, 'Welcome home son, job well done.'"

The church was a cacophony. Father O'Boyle hit the nerve and hit it hard. The entire congregation was celebrating the life of a truly great man, the only way they could with their raw emotions. They exited the church, went to the cemetery, bade Tim goodbye, and ended the day with a luncheon paid by Mickey at the Greenleaf. Later that week, Mickey moved from the apartment on Webster Avenue to Tim's apartment. He used Webster Avenue for betting and hired three guys to work shifts taking action. With the contents of the bank deposit box and the apartment safe, his future was secure and that was the last gift Tim gave him.

4
Ma Bell

Each morning, Mickey O went to The Widow's Walk, just so he could talk with Duke Callahan about topics other than gambling. These conversations were always pleasant. They varied, some days social and political, other days just storytelling by Duke. It was always Duke's unusual venture into the humorous that had him attentively listening to each and every tale. Mickey repeatedly stated, "You should write a book."

This was the last of these days with Duke sheepishly stating, "I don't want to sound corny, but I am going to miss these morning meetings."

"Duke, I have to go where the money is. O'Brien is going to open a fancy restaurant and bar in Riverdale. That's where the rich Irish money is. He wants me to open up shop there; it's an opportunity I have to take advantage of."

"Well, I guess the phone here won't be all that busy without you at the helm."

"Don't worry, Duke. The boys can get their action in at my new number or the apartment."

Duke responded sadly, "Well, I'm gonna miss you, kid."

"Duke, I'm gonna be the big kahuna now. You and I will be having dinner so often, it could turn into an affair."

MICKEY O   DUKE CALLAHAN

As the front door opened, in came Logan sporting an unusual bounce to his step.

Gruffly, he stated, "Good morning, you two assholes."

Duke queried, "What caused you to get up on the right side of the bed today? I'm not used to seeing an actual, happy morning Logan."

Logan snapped back, "If you want to know, I'm working on something that could turn out good for the old asshole."

Amusingly, Duke replied, "Well, at least you know how to describe yourself, old and an asshole."

Logan replied, "Well, aren't you the comedian."

Officiously Duke said, "Enough of this small talk, get the ice for the bar and take inventory of the booze."

"Up yours, dickhead. I'm not going to do a thing until I get my tea and a bagel."

Five minutes later, Duke obediently submitted to Logan's request and went to Frank's Deli and came back with the goods.

Logan frowned as he peered into his tea container. "How many times do I have to tell you, don't fill the cup to the top." He dumped out half the tea and replaced it with three fingers of Fleischman's Rye.

Duke shook his head, "You are a beauty, Logan."

Instantaneously, the three men burst into laughter. Duke's mischievous side had been tickled. He knew from Logan's demeanor that there was a mother load of ball busting to be discovered. He, the Duke, would unearth it with just a little time and effort.

Logan finally set up shop for the day and his shift transpired as usual; ball busting on steroids and "assholes" being hurled in all directions.

Six p.m. arrived and Duke was Logan's relief. He was working for Moose Morano, the steady Friday night bartender, who had a family function to attend.

Logan was now planted on the customers side and queried, "Where's my Manhattan, asshole? And make sure it's made right."

Duke acknowledged the request, but it wasn't the drink on his mind. He wanted to know what made Logan so giddy this morning. When he finds out, he would pounce all over Logan and immerse his pal in a sea of misery.

It didn't take long for the first clue to be revealed. Logan was just about to use the pay phone as Jimmy Feeley got to the phone a second before Logan.

It ignited an instant outburst, "Hey, asshole, I want to use the phone, how long are you going to be?"

"Relax, I won't be that long." Feeley replied.

Light bulbs were going off in Duke's head. Logan had just peeled off the first layer of this mystery. He needed that phone ASAP. Duke was going to have some fun until all the layers were peeled away.

Duke meandered to the other side of the bar, where a second phone was located that enabled the bartender to answer the phone

DUKE   DUKE + LOGAN

without leaving the bar area. The catch to the situation, when you lift the secondary phone, the person attempting to make a call doesn't get a dial tone, therefore he can't make a call. Simple as it may be, it spelled disaster for Logan.

Feeley finally finished his call and received the required asshole' as Logan lifted the receiver. Duke, with perfect timing, lifted the bar phone, which caused the pay phone to be inoperable.

Logan elevated his usual gruff voice with a resounding. What the fuck is wrong with this phone, asshole?"

Duke gave Logan the I don't have a clue look.

"Why don't you try again, Jimmy?"

Logan silently lifted the receiver and tried again. No tone again.

Duke had perfect timing, "Jimmy, why don't you wait a few minutes? Maybe it's just a glitch and the dial tone will return."

"Return this asshole, make me another Manhattan," as Logan returned to his seat.

While he was making a drink for Logan, the phone rang and Duke grabbed the pay phone.

"Widow's Walk. Who? Willy it's for you, it's your brother Daniel."

Duke returned to the opposite end of the bar and strategically stationed himself next to the secondary phone. Willy got off the phone as Logan slowly left his seat again. Duke turned his eyes upward and said a silent, "Thank you, God."

Logan approached the pay phone and lifted the receiver. Simultaneously Duke lifted his receiver and once again: dead air, no dial tone. Eruption commenced. Logan was past the usual, "asshole." Obscenities of all sorts were rolling off his tongue.

Duke struck gold. The sharpies in the bar knew it was a caper orchestrated by the Duke. The chuckling turned to laughter which lifted Logan to a higher level of bonkers. Logan was hyperventilating, so he returned to his drink to calm down.

Eddie Washinki bore a striking resemblance to Logan, hence the nickname, Son of Logan. Eddie went to the pay phone, put in a dime and started to dial. Logan's look was one of bewilderment.

"What's that, Mom, you need a quart of milk and a loaf of bread? I'll be leaving in half an hour and will stop at Frank's Deli."

Eddie hung up and Duke, still situated by the secondary phone, said the words that would ignite the bar into laughter.

"Jimmy, even Son of Logan was able to use the phone. It must be your touch, you are probably too rough on the phone, therefore, no dial tone."

Expressions of delight were heard from the patrons.

Logan shouts out a universal, "You're all a bunch of assholes."

Duke encountered a small dilemma knowing the phone was only a part of Logan's mysterious demeanor. He realized he had to know the entire story to be able to deliver the most misery for Logan. Duke approached the phone, lifted the receiver, put in a dime, and presto, dial tone!

"Here, Jimmy, dial away!"

Logan dialed his number and spoke in a hushed tone. The call was short and ended with Jimmy saying, "I'll ask him if it's all right."

Logan hung up and asked Duke if he could speak with him in the kitchen.

Logan knew Mickey O wasn't going to use the pay phone for action anymore. He wanted to know if he could take horse bets and numbers called in from a bar in Rockaway. Logan continued, his partner was going to be the day bartender, Mamie. She would call in the action periodically so I could keep track.

"Duke, it's not going to be a lot of bets. It wouldn't distract me from the bar and it would keep me in Manhattan money."

This was music to Duke's ears, his plan now took shape. He only had to nail down the specifics.

The obvious one was stated by Duke, "Jimmy, the only problem might be the phone itself, you saw what happened today."

Logan replied, "Yeah, only a dipshit like you would have a phone that doesn't work, just like your brain asshole."

This assessment elated Duke because it had ridden him of any sort of guilty conscience connected to the wrath he was about to inflict on Logan.

"Nice talk, Jimmy, I'm going to show you, I'm the better person. I'm going to work your shift tomorrow, so you can concentrate on your new business. I'll come in extra early to make sure the phone is operable. If it isn't, I'll call the phone company and they should be able to send a repairman."

Logan was taken back, "You know you're not that bad for an asshole. Thanks for helping me out."

"Jimmy, anytime. After all, as the saying goes, what are friends for if not to help each other out?"

Logan finished his drink and with an energetic spring to his step, turned around and bade everyone farewell as he exited The Walk, looking forward to the next day.

Duke arrived at the bar by 7:30 a.m. Saturday morning to implement his plan. He went to the pay phone. He lifted the receiver and twisted off the couplings that held the hearing and speaking components. He reversed the speaker and hearing components and screwed on the couplings. He had created a phone that still worked, but the mechanics of hearing and speaking had now become quite complicated.

At 8:30, Duke called Mickey O to see if the phone would produce the intended consequences. Duke had the usual talking part to his ear and upon hearing his friend, he quickly situated the hearing end to his mouth. As he spoke to Mickey, he resembled Sinatra ready to belt out a tune. He told Mickey to come to the bar before he went to Riverdale. Duke chuckled and promised it would be worth his while. He maneuvered the phone again to listen to Mickey's response. Mickey ended the conversation by telling Duke he would be there by ten a.m.

Duke hung up and smiled at the same time Logan arrived. He was satisfied. With this simple maneuver, he reversed the operation required to make a call.

Mickey O arrived ahead of schedule. Logan barked at Mickey to get him a tea and bagel. Ninety-nine percent of people that talked to Mickey that way would receive the required, "Go fuck yourself." Logan was in the one percent which amused Mickey and he did as told.

Duke noticed that Logan's face was beaming, as he walked past the early blasters, the a.m. shots and beers gang. He thought with a weathered face like Logan, it was unbelievable that he actually looked more youthful. That look would eventually fade away within the next half hour.

Duke, upon seeing the rejuvenated Logan, was suddenly struck with a pang of conscience. Maybe, he shouldn't fulfill this caper, however the old Duke came through. Subconsciously he was smacked in his face by his inner Duke. His devil side said, "Are you fucking crazy? This escapade will go down into neighborhood folklore. It will be passed down from one generation to the next. Now get back to work and that's an order!"

Duke shook off this pang of self-imposed guilt and went back to the plan. He would let Logan enjoy his tea with whiskey and his bagel before informing him of the phone problem. The three morning patrons were oblivious of what was about to occur. Methodically, they sipped their shots and guzzled their beers. This tranquil setting would diminish when Duke informed Logan of the phone problem.

After he told Logan, Mickey O's ears perked up and the other three imbibers had their attentions drawn to Duke.

Logan replied, "What's the problem with the phone? I hope it's not out of service, knowing you, asshole, that could be the case."

"Jimmy, there's just a minor maneuver you have to master, after which everything will be easy peasy."

Logan's face reddened, "Easy peasy, my ass, tell me the fucking problem."

Duke explained, "Jimmy, I had the phone guy come in at about eight a.m. and he said the problem yesterday and today was the receiver. It has to be replaced, but he couldn't come back with a new receiver til Monday."

"So?" Logan with a quizzical look asked.

Duke had the phone in his hand, "Jimmy, watch me carefully." He put the listening end of the phone two inches from his mouth. "You see, Jim, you have to speak into the listening end and after speaking, you have to quickly transfer the receiver to your ear with the end you usually speak into. It's really quite simple."

"You, fucking asshole." Logans face was now crimson. This could only happen to a nimrod like you and now you are bringing me down."

"Jimmy, relax!"

Logan snapped back, "Relax! You're fucking telling me to relax. I should go into the kitchen, get a softball bat and shove it up your ass."

A composed Duke, tells our boy, "Jim, you don't have to be so harsh. This is a minor difficulty, that we both can overcome together." Spoken like a typical politician, the Duke continued, "Jim, let's do a dry run on how you will operate the receiver at noon time, ready?"

"Why the fuck does this shit always happen to me?"

"Now, Jimmy let's not play victim."

Mickey O was ready to bust a gut, but he kept a cool demeanor as he observed Duke's tutorial. He told Jimmy, "Just listen to Duke, he wouldn't steer you wrong, he has only the best intentions for you. After all, what are friends for?"

Logan's head swiveled like a scene from the "Exorcist". Now facing Mickey, he said, "Another asshole heard from. If you didn't get so greedy, you never would have went to Riverdale. You'd be here and I wouldn't be pleasantly fucked like I am now."

"You're welcome," replied Mickey.

Duke got Logan's attention again and began the lesson, "Jimmy, we'll make believe the phone is ringing. You will lift the receiver. Remember, when you speak, you must bring the listening end to your mouth and pretend you are singing a Sinatra song, but instead of singing you just say, hello."

"Gimme the phone, asshole."

"No," replied Duke, "we'll place it on the hook."

"Now I know what hell is going to be like," Logan snidely remarked.

"Ready Jim, the phone is ringing."

Logan hesitated.

"You have to think on your feet, Jim. Remember, the more smoothly you react, the better you can handle this minor set back."

Logan screamed, "Fuck you," as small drops of spittle exited his mouth.

"Now Jim, keep your composure. OK, the phone is ringing."

Logan removed the receiver and surprisingly spoke into the hearing end as he said, "Hello." He left the phone in that same position for five seconds, not realizing that he can't hear a thing unless he transferred the speaking end to his ear.

Duke admonished Logan, "Jimmy, after hello, you have to immediately, I mean pronto, maneuver the receiver so you can hear Mamie give you the action." "

All right, all right," said Logan.

"Ok, put the receiver on the hook. The phone is now ringing," directed Duke.

Logan gave him the look of an assassin. He removed the receiver, said hello into the hearing end, and quickly transferred the speaking end to his ear which enabled him to listen.

"Well done, Jimmy."

The only physical trait missing from our hero was smoke coming out of his ears. The face was red like you could cook a burger on it and spittle was drooling from his mouth. With the gentle body shake of a mambo dancer, he appeared to be a human volcano. Logan was quiet, but seething. Duke said he would go next door to Frank's Deli and call The Walk from Frank's pay phone, staging a dress rehearsal. As Duke greeted Frank, he went to the payphone and called Mike Paxton. He told Mike to call all the crew to come to The Walk and enjoy what was to be an epic comedic event. Duke hung up and called The Walk. Logan answered, but in the usual manner; he had forgotten Duke's instructions already.

Duke quickly exited Frank's. As he entered The Walk, he admonished Logan.

What's wrong with you, Jimmy? I showed you the proper mechanics for answering the phone and you forgot them."

"Mechanics," answered Logan. "Mechanics! I'll give you mechanics! Along with that softball bat, I'll shove a wrench up your ass! You're acting like I'm the one who screwed up the phone. Well, let me tell you, moron, it's your phone. So it's you that fucked it up!"

Duke answered, "Now, Jimmy, temper, temper. Remember, you must keep calm. You must take control of the situation and not have the situation control you."

Logan screamed again, "Control the situation? All of a sudden, you're a psychiatrist, you just about made it out of Saint Brendan's grammar school. All right, Dr. Callahan, let's rehearse what you call, 'The Mechanics,' again."

One more time, they did the basic ABC's. Duke went to Frank's to call again.

The Walk's phone rang several times. When Logan answered, Duke heard Logan's melodic voice, "Hello, asshole."

Duke replied, "Ok, Jimmy, you should be listening now. So repeat after me. I will not panic, I will remain calm."

There was no response. Duke hung up and called again.

Logan, in a perpetual state of misery, answered in a soft depressed tone, "Is this you, asshole? Why did you hang up on me?"

Like a shot, Mickey O chimed in, "You didn't shift the phone like Duke instructed."

"Another lunatic heard from. I'm being schooled by not one, but two dipshits."

As the phone rang, once more Logan lifted the receiver and placed the receiving end to his ear. He heard Duke tell him he had to be quicker with the one two procedure.

Logan goes to the ultimate octave of screaming. "Why does shit like this always happen to me."

Mickey O answered, "I guess you are one of those people who has luck, but it's bad luck."

Logan responded, "Is that right, Socrates? Holy shit! How many morons can I be surrounded by?"

Mickey O and the shots and beers gang started to chuckle as Duke entered The Walk.

"Now Jimmy, you seem to have the basics down, but you just have to increase the tempo. Like this, mouth to ear. One, two, one, two."

Logan was beside himself. As he looked around, he became the joke of a bunch of losers.

"I've hit bottom; I can't go any lower. I am the laughing stock of some whacked out bookie and these screaming alcoholics, none of which can spell their own names. They laugh; they mock. This is just the beginning of one of the worst days of my life, all because of nimrod and his screwed up phone."

The door to The Walk opened and in came Danny Walsh, Mike Paxton, the Cozzi brothers, Jim Feeley, Matty Kirby, Willy Dealy, Ray Quigley, and Moose Morano. In a controlled tone, Logan questioned the group.

"Why are you assholes here? It's eleven a.m. You're supposed to be playing basketball in the school yard?"

Moose Morano told Logan, "The weather's not that great, so we took a pass."

Logan snapped back, "Idiot, it's eighty degrees and not a cloud in the sky."

Feeley answered, "Well, Jimmy, that shows how much you follow the weather. Mr. Weatherbee of ABC News said there was a mean weather pattern that will arrive early this afternoon. We figured, why not visit our favorite bartender with that endearing personality?"

Logan grunted and turned his attention back to the phone dilemma. Duke was right behind Logan with receiver in hand.

"Jimmy, I've come up with a great way for you to master this reverse phone situation."

"Please tell me, oh great one. Let me hear these pearls of wisdom."

The bar was so quiet, one could hear the proverbial pin drop. Everyone present, even the a.m. alcoholics, knew Duke was ready to unleash hell.

"Jimmy, I'm sure you've seen those movies with Jimmy Stewart as a squadron leader in World War II. He spoke to his crew similar to the way you have to hold the phone when answering a call. We've gone over this before, the usual listening end will be brought down to your mouth just like Jimmy Stewart. So instead of thinking 'one,' you'll envision Stewart as a squadron leader and say, Jimmy Stewart, instead of 'one.' Remember, Jim, don't say 'one,' say, 'Jimmy Stewart.'"

Logan looked at Duke as if he had two heads. He replied, "Listen, doofus, I was in World War II and I also saw Jimmy Stewart movies about World War II. Where does it say, that I say 'Jimmy Stewart,' instead of simply saying, 'one?' How does that simplify answering this shit hook phone?"

Duke quickly jumped in, "Jimmy, 'One' is just that. 'One' is very blah, very blah. 'Jimmy Stewart' gives you the advantage of word association and in that vein we have just the right phrase for two.'"

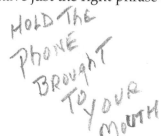

Jimmy snapped, "What pray tell might that be, dickhead?"

"Jim, from your Catholic upbringing, you understand the religious implications of Easter, but there are the commercial aspects. Jimmy, can you tell me what you look forward to during the Easter celebration?"

Silence, once again, took over the bar.

Logan said, "You know what would tickle me pink during the Easter holiday? Me kicking your ass."

"Now, now, Jimmy Boy. It can't always be about you."

Logan, screamed, "Always about me? When the fuck is it ever about me? You mean when it's hell on earth then it's about me."

Sounds of laughter trickled down the bar as the crowd had swelled to twenty-three patrons.

Duke pressed on, "Jimmy, what do children want most on Easter Sunday?"

Logan answered Duke, as if Duke were his eighth grade teacher in Saint Brendan's, "Well, Easter eggs, Easter egg hunts, ah... ah..."

Duke prompted Logan. "Jimmy, how about peeps? The tiny yellow marshmallow chicks?"

A frustrated Logan said, "Peeps, how was I supposed to know peeps? I'd like to shove a dozen peeps down your throat."

"There you go again, remember, violence is not the answer."

The bar erupted in laughter, reminiscent of the canned laughter used responding to some stale joke in a half hour sitcom.

Duke
Eighth
GRADE
Teacher

The laughter was not canned, but bust your gut laughter. Each man restrained himself because he didn't want to disturb the dialogue between these two combatants. No, a disruption may hinder the flow of comedic intention. They were quite the obedient audience and Duke knew that.

"Jimmy, you're leaving out the most obvious treat that children consume on Easter Sunday. It's made of chocolate. Come on, Jim, you know what it is."

"Give me a hint."

Duke had Logan hook, line, and sinker.

"It's a cute little animal that universally signifies the Easter celebration."

"A rabbit, a rabbit, that's it."

"Yes, Jimmy, it's a rabbit, but we don't call it a rabbit."

Duke coaxed Logan towards the answer. Logan, with a bewildered look puts his thinking cap on, but still no answer.

"Bunny, Jim, it's the Easter Bunny."

"What the hell is the difference? Rabbit, bunny, they're both the same."

There was controlled laughter after each back and forth.

"Jimmy, it will always be the Easter Bunny. Children ask their parents, where's the chocolate Easter bunny? Your children wanted the Easter Bunny, not the Easter Rabbit."

"OK, imbecile, Easter Bunny, does that make you happy? By the way, what the fuck does the Easter Bunny have to do with this dilemma I am in?"

Duke chided, "Language, Jim, do you always have to use profanity?"

With his face reddening by the minute, Logan said, "OK, if it makes you feel better. Oh, kind sir, I fail to see the difference of one saying, Easter Rabbit as opposed to the nomenclature Easter Bunny? Dipshit."

Duke replied, "Very impressive. Now back to the matter at hand. What's the most noticeable physical trait of the Easter Bunny?"

"Enough with the questions," Logan replied, "It's 11:40 and the action will be coming in at noon. The answer is his ears."

Duke smiled, "Correct, Jimmy, it's the bunny's ears, very good. You understand why we are talking about the Easter Bunny's ears."

"No, I have no idea why we are talking about some asshole Bunny's ears."

"Well, Jimmy, after you answered the phone, mentally envisioning Jimmy Stewart; you then place the speaking end to your ear and the receiver looked like a bunny ear coming out of your head."

Logan screamed, "Holy shit, how did you come up with this one? Bunny ear? I am just sinking in a sea of misery."

"Now, we have made sure that there is no mechanical mixup which was quite evident with 'One' and 'Two.' The replacement is word association with the answering and listening process. When speaking you envision Jimmy Stewart addressing

NOMENCLATURE

66

the squadron with his hand held mic and listening you envision bunny ear. To repeat, no more 'One' and 'Two.' Now it's 'Jimmy Stewart' and 'bunny ear.' Once again, 'Jimmy Stewart. Bunny ear.'"

Logan, exasperated, resigned himself to this insane situation.

Duke commanded, "What do you say, Jimmy?"

Logan, dejected and in a depressed voice repeated, "Jimmy Stewart. Bunny ear."

Duke smiled, "That's good, Jimmy, very good. Now remember, you don't have to voice those associations. Just mentally associate with answering and listening. If you get confused, we'll remind you with the proper verbal designations. Example, you hesitate answering, we'll yell out 'Jimmy Stewart.' And we'll yell out 'bunny ear' if there is a delay in listening."

It was 11:50 a.m. and the bar totaled thirty patrons. All of them, pleasantly high on booze and beer and well aware of the situation. There was no laughter, just various muffled conversations. Everyone was waiting for the phone to ring. Mickey O was so caught up in the situation that he directed one of his associates to open shop in Riverdale. No way was he going to miss this play. Even though the bar clock was silent in keeping time, everyone had their eyes on it and were mentally tick-tocking their way to noon. One minute, fifty seconds, thirty seconds, ten, nine, eight, seven, six, five, four, three, two, one. Ring, ring, ring.

Logan screwed up and answered the phone the proper way. "Hello. Hello."

On the other side you could actually hear Mamie's voice. It was a shrill combination of Edith Bunker and Carol Channing, "Jimeee! Jimeee!"

The bar shouted out, "Jimmy Stewart," But it was too late, Mamie hung up.

Coach Callahan was there for support. "Jimmy remember, 'Jimmy Stewart. Bunny ear.'"

"Shut up," yells Logan.

The entire bar was packed within hearing distance. They were actually suffocating Logan. If he was claustrophobic, he would have made a mad dash out of The Walk. Everyone anticipated the ringing pay phone and in thirty second they were not disappointed.

Logan quickly removed the phone. Duke was quietly prompting him, "Jimmy Stewart, Jimmy Stewart." Before Jimmy spoke, he shot Duke an, "If looks could kill" glance and said, "Mamie."

You heard that piercing voice once again, "Jimeee! Jimeee!" Why? Because Logan reverted back to the usual manner of holding the phone.

The crowd yelled a cacophony of, "Bunny ear, bunny ear."

Then another shriek, "Jimeee! Jimeee!" After which, the dial tone returned when Mamie hung up again.

Mickey O, now on his third bloody Mary, led a chorus of thirty men, all of them making the required hand imitations shouting, "Jimmy Stewart. Bunny ear." The chant rose to a deafening crescendo as the mimicking of the hand movement to the mouth, accompanied by a resounding, "Jimmy Stewart." Then the hand to the ear, "Bunny ear."

After three more choruses, Logan had had it. "Shut the fuck up!" He heaped his wrath on one person, you guessed it Duke. Logan, with the voice of a beaten man, "You asshole, this happened because of you. Why the fuck can't anything go my way?"

Duke interjected, "Jimmy, I cant help it that the phone is screwed up. I'm only here to make sure everything goes smoothly for you."

Logan screamed, "Go smoothly? You call this going smoothly?"

Mickey O stepped up and said, "Jimmy, all the boys know the proper mechanics, so when you get confused, we are here to help you. Just shoot us a glance and our hands will be in the proper position. It will be like learning the ABC's again. Once you have mastered the repetition of these two hand motions, you'll conquer your mental block. After all, Jim, it's really not all that difficult."

Logan stammered, "Listen doofus, if it's so easy, why don't you man the phone and take the bets?"

Mickey O interrupted, "Listen, Jimmy, you wanted to be a bookie, this is just part of the territory you have to deal with. Remember the phrase, we shall overcome, just substitute I for we."

Logan was ready to pounce on Mickey, but the phone rang. He quickly grabbed the receiver and brought it down to the Jimmy Stewart, and screamed, "Hello, Mamie." He quickly attempted to reposition the phone to "bunny ear," but lost control of the receiver in transition.

Again, "Jimeee! Jimeee! I can't hear you." Logan fitfully attempted to control the receiver, but it swung aimlessly like a horse thief hung from an oak tree. Finally, it was in his grasp, but there was no Mamie, just a dial tone.

He looked up and everyone had their hand attached to their right ear. In his mind, it was all over; the cockiness he had at eleven a.m. had dissipated to a self imposed defeat. He was just about ready to give up.

Duke came to the rescue, "Jimmy, why don't you call Mamie? I think that's what's needed to right the USS Logan. It should eliminate the confusion."

Logan was ready to say something obnoxious, but he relented. He said, "Asshole, that's the first sensible thing that came out of your dumb ass mouth today."

Duke wryly smiled as Jimmy put the dime in the pay phone.

Logan did the bunny ear and again the piercing voice, "Killeen's Bar." He glanced at the bar and all patrons were mimicking the proper phone position. He immediately shot down to the Jimmy Stewart.

Logan told Mamie, "It's 12:15 and the first race goes off at 12:30." He inquired how many bets she had taken. Back to the bunny ear, perfect timing.

Mamie still "Jimeee! Jimeee! Jimeee!"

Logan still stuck at bunny ear starts yelling, "I'm here, I'm fucking here."

"Jimeee, there's something wrong with the phone," and hung up one more time.

Logan lost it. He started pounding the phone with the receiver. Duke and Mickey stepped in to restrain him.

Duke said, "Relax, Jim, calm down, it's you that screwed up not the poor phone."

Logan looked at Duke and his merry band and they all shook their heads in disappointment. To a man, they had their right hands in the Jimmy Stewart position.

Mickey chimed in and said, "Listen, Logan, any moron can so this. I am sick and tired of this Jimmy Stewart, bunny ear routine. Buck up, master it, or just go home to Mommy. Now listen. We won't call out the positions you are supposed to be at. We'll just do the hand motions. Am I making myself clear? Listen to us, we are here to help you. Now dial the God-damn number."

Duke played good cop to Mickey's bad cop. He offered another suggestion. "Jim, tell Mamie to count to three before she speaks to you, that will give you more than enough time to reposition the phone."

Logan replied, "I can't believe it asshole, that's your second sensible thought today."

Duke smiled and Logan dialed away.

Mamie answered, "Killeen's bar."

Logan was in the Jimmy Stewart position and the whole bar was acting in tandem with him. Logan said, "Mamie, I want you to count to three, so I can reposition the phone."

She immediately started to talk unbelievably louder. Yeah, that's right she was screaming. "Why do I have to count to three, Jimeee?"

Logan started to yell, but the receiver was in the bunny ear position because he was looking at all the lunatics not saying a word, but having their right hands to their ears. This resulted in Logan still having the phone sticking up right in his ear as he started talking.

"Mamie, just do as I say. It's ten minutes to post time, now do you understand why you have to count to three."

Total silence. Logan could hear her perfectly and he was so irate that spittle started to eject from his mouth.

"You count to three and then I will be able to hear, because as I said before, it gives me time to reposition." He viewed the bar and saw the boys doing the Jimmy Stewart. The problem arose again because while he explained the procedure, there was no-one home.

"Jimeee, all I heard was reposition. I'll call you," and Mamie hung up before Logan could get to the Jimmy Stewart.

Seven minutes to post time and Logan didn't have a clue who bet or what type of bets have been made. The phone rings. Everyone was doing the Jimmy Stewart. Logan did likewise.

"Listen, Mamie, don't ask why you have to count to three. It has to do with my repositioning."

Logan followed the lunatics to the bunny ear. Mamie inquired, "What's this repositioning, are you moving furniture?"

Logan, back to the Stewart said, "I am not moving fucking furniture, there is something wrong with this asshole's phone."

Back to bunny ear, Mamie, answered, "Who's Mr. Asshole? I just don't understand."

Logan, back to the Stewart, "His name is not Mr. Asshole. It's Duke, and he is the owner of this den of misery. Stop asking questions, Just do as I said before, count to three and then talk."

Logan repositioned to the bunny ear. All he heard was "One, two, three," and then Mamie said, "I don't hear you Jimeee."

Logan, from the bunny ear position, screamed into the stale bar air, "You're not supposed to hear, you're supposed to give me the bets."

The dial tone again.

Logan had had it, "The dumb bitch hung up again. I'm getting blisters on my forefinger from dialing this scumbag phone."

Four minutes til post time. Logan was so infuriated that he attacked Duke with his arthritic hands clinched around his throat. Mickey had to pry the fingers from Duke's neck.

Logan repeatedly screamed, "I'm gonna kill you, you ruined my life."

Mickey O and Walsh looked at each other in amazement. Mentally, they both agreed. This was one strong little bastard as they eventually got him under control. Logan was now destroyed.

Yes, he came into The Walk with a confident strut, dressed to the nines. Now, he melted and crumbled to the filthy bar floor. His fedora was five feet from him. His hair, which stuck up Alfalfa style in all directions, was matted with sweat. His eyes were filled with tears of a psychotic murderer and his mouth foamed like some rabid dog. Mickey O, without speaking, shot a sympathetic glance at Duke. Duke understood.

He extended his hand to Logan and lifted him from the floor. This shattered image was now in front of him and elicited a wave of compassion from the Duke. That's right, he was going to let Logan off the hook. He'd open an escape hatch from the misery and despair which hopefully would bring back the old Logan.

Sympathetically, Duke said, "Jimmy, it's two minutes to post. I'll call Mamie and take all the bets."

A hunched over Logan, replied, "Really asshole? You'll do this for me?"

Without hesitating, Duke nodded his head in the affirmative., He grabbed the receiver, twisted off both ends, and reversed the components, restoring their original places.

Logan was physically and emotionally spent. He couldn't even muster the strength to go to the kitchen, get a bat, and blast

Duke's head. This was a once in a lifetime event for Logan; he was speechless and motionless.

Weakly, he cried out, "Why? Why?" He meekly inquired, "Did my family, many generations ago, screw over your family in some shit hole village in Ireland, that caused you to constantly stick me with a revenge needle as if I were your personal voodoo doll."

"No, Jimmy," answered Duke, "you just happen to have a close friend who has a sick and, some would say, demented sense of humor."

Logan nodded his head slowly in agreement.

Mickey O rushed to the phone and grabbed it from Duke. He called Mamie and with the assistance of one of her patrons was able to get all the early bets down with thirty seconds to spare. Mickey ran the show for the remainder of the day.

You see, Logan was after all a shattered man. He doubled up on the Manhattans and was a mumbling drunk one hour after the first race. He was exhibiting a full blown case of the shakes and bakes. You would have thought he was the main character in "The Days of Wine and Roses." His sullen demeanor sapped his perennial pervasive nature. The Walk was cooled by air conditioning, but beads of sweat single filed the way down his forehead and onto his nose where they would swan dive one by one into his drink. The sweat infused Manhattans would be transported to his quivering lips by two shaking hands. We thought a straight jacket would be needed.

This was not necessary for Logan gently placed his head on the bar and slipped into a blissful sleep. He awoke when all the days action had been taken by Mickey O. After comparing the results of the bets taken, Logan was on the plus side. Logan, now groggy, was informed that everything went smoothly. Uncharacteristically, he thanked Mickey O in a low humbled toned voice.

He turned to Duke and reverted back to his old self, "You really did it to me this time."

Duke interrupted him and contritely said, "Jimmy, I am truly sorry for doing this to you. I never thought it would get so crazy."

Duke approached Logan and gave him a big bear hug.

With the apology and hug over, Logan said with a smile, "You know you're still an asshole, but in a strange way you love me. Unfortunately, these capers will never stop, so do me a favor. Don't send me to the doors of hell again."

Duke smiled and nodded in the affirmative, "Never again, Jimmy."

Duke told Mickey and Logan that they all were going to Connolly's Steakhouse on his dime. As Mickey gave the OK sign, Logan said, "Thanks for the apology dinner."

All three laughed loudly, as they exited The Walk on their way to Connolly's.

Sadly, Logan's gambling venture ended three weeks later when one of his customers hit a three digit number that paid six hundred to one. The bettor had ten dollars on it which caused Logan to lose six thousand dollars, money he didn't have.

Enter, Mickey O to the rescue. He floated Logan the six grand telling him, "Jimmy, this bartending bookie combo is not working well for you. You don't have enough capital to cover big losses and that's not good. I'll pay your man the six thousand and you'll give all your players my new Riverdale number and I'll take all their action. I'll put you on a half sheet and you'll be in the red for six thousand."

He told Logan that he would have to work off the six thousand dollars in order to get back to even. After which, whatever the customers would lose they would split fifty-fifty. Logan had two choices: he would either go to HFC Loan Company to take out an eighteen-percent interest loan or go with the deal Mickey offered. Logan realized that it could possibly be a while before he gets back to even, but it eliminated the financial stress. So he agreed to Mickey O's proposition.

Jimmy eventually got out of the hole and he and Mickey had a profitable relationship for years to come. This kept Logan in Manhattans and steak dinner money. It was a deal made with a firm handshake, no lawyer, no written contract. That's part of the fabric of the neighborhood. Your word is your bond.

DANNY HOFER

5
Tickets, But No Play

Saint Brendan's was a neighborhood that had their revered lions. Guys that put the emphasize on "tough" when you mention "tough guys." They never looked for trouble. They never bragged about how tough they were, or reminded you that they could kick your ass whenever they pleased. The fact was, they were the opposite: mild mannered, tons of personality, and their last resort would be turning to fisticuffs. One would believe by this type of personality mirage that these warriors could be had. Those who would be mislead into believing such folly, would be on a journey over a bridge with no possible return. For when the anger match had been lit, the onslaught would be unstoppable. Each of these men would face any foe and odds were that they would end up victorious.

Neil Conlin was such a man.

It was the second Saturday of August, 1970. The weather was unbearable, ninety degrees with high humidity. Neil was in his apartment on Hull Avenue, dressed in white boxer shorts and a tee shirt. He sat comfortably by the fan in his favorite easy chair. Three little gifts from God, sons ages two to five, where putting forth their best macho image imitating their favorite cowboys with their six shooters blazing. Neil's wife Noreen was taking a break from the madness as she sipped a glass of ice tea at the kitchen table. As the shootout at the OK Corral intensified, the ringing phone was almost ignored, but Noreen heard it on its fourth ring.

"Hello," Noreen answered, "Oh, Jack. How's everything with you?"

It was Jack Houlihan from the neighborhood, but now relocated to lower Manhattan so he could be near his newly started accounting firm.

Jack replied, "It can't be much better, Noreen. The business is slowly improving and I have scheduled a few meetings with prospective clients."

Noreen exclaimed, "Oh, that's great Jack! I'll get Neil. Good luck and goodbye."

Noreen voiced an extra loud, "Neil!" to overcome the western mayhem. "It's Jack Houlihan, honey."

Neil slowly made his way to the phone, stepping over the dinette table, now on its side and christened Fort Conlin. He gently nudged one of the combatants to the side as he entered the kitchen. Noreen handed him the phone along with a soft peck on the cheek.

"Hi, Jack, what's up?"

"Well, Neil, old friend, it couldn't be much better as I mentioned to Noreen. In the coming month, I am having several meetings with prospective clients, that will double my business if successful. Neil, this could be good for the both of us. Instead of giving legal work to you piecemeal, we might have to set up a different arrangement; one that would result in your being hired on salary to handle the firms legal affairs."

Neil's eyes lit up, "Geez Jack, that would be great. Having a steady income would allow me the possibility of going from a solo practice to the formation of my own law firm."

Neil knew that he would have to dedicate a great deal of time to Jack's enterprise, but with his younger brother Mike graduating law school in January, he would be able to hire him for legal matters that he couldn't undertake. Putting his brother on salary would guarantee the success of his fledging law firm. Neil was envisioning these possibilities as Jack carried on his one way conversation.

He snapped back to reality when he heard Jack say, "Hey, Neil, just one other matter. I know you set up a dinner and theater date for September 14th and I appreciate you putting on the Ritz for me. You want to show your appreciation for my hiring you. Neil, you're a dear friend and the money you'll spend that night, well, you have three little ones and one more on the way. You should use that money for the Conlin clan. Also, buddy, with these possibilities coming around so rapidly, I hope to be booked up every day in the near future. The prospect of me not being able to enjoy myself that night could be a fifty-fifty shot. I'll make you a deal, cancel the 14th and if the plans for my company come to fruition, I'll take you out for a dinner date on December 15th".

Neil shot back, "Listen, Jack, we'll make it December 15th, but it's still the original arrangement. Saturday matinee of Guys and Dolls, and Connolly's Steakhouse after the show, but I pay. Are we straight with that? A day of celebration for you, me, Jeannie, and Noreen, no matter which way the cards fall, I pay."

Jack meekly agreed.

He knew his friend only too well. The two of them were carbon copies of a certain Irish breed. Both were six-foot-one with ebony black hair, brown eyes, and a bit of a Mediterranean look about them. They both had mischievous grins with Neil having accompanying dimples. This type of Irish was supposedly from the Spanish Armada survivors ending up in Ireland. Whatever it was, the two were such look a likes, they were often mistaken for brothers. Intelligence and humor were the hallmarks of their personalities, but only one had the fight in him and Jack knew it wasn't him. There were many a time when Jack saw his friend fight the righteous battle and come out the victor. Therefore, he knew that Neil's final declaration was just that, final. So, December 15th, he and his wife were to be guests of the Conlin's. Jack ended, "Ok, Neil, we celebrate on December 15th and you pay. Thanks." They both chuckled as they ended the conversation.

Neil hung up, turned towards his wife and playfully grabbed her as they danced with no music. The boys took notice, stopped the battle and sprinted to their parents. There it was, all five Conlins hugging and doing a "Good Night My Love," slow dance which was sung by that great Irish tenor, Neil Conlin. Neil was overwhelmed as he held Noreen and the kids. He so loved his sons, but Noreen always took his breathe away and made his heart flutter. His love for her had no bounds. The five-foot-five, freckled-face, strawberry-blonde with sky-blue eyes and the look of an angel had captured his heart from day one. He knew he would be her love prisoner for eternity.

Neil's singing ended and the boys unfastened themselves and went back to saving the West. Neil loosened his grip on Noreen and as he looked at her beaming face, gave her a soft love kiss while whispering that he had to make a phone call. As Neil turned towards the phone, Noreen playfully pinched his rear accompanied by a teenage giggle.

"Aren't we the fresh one," stated a blushing Neil as he dialed the phone.

Noreen sexily pouted her lips and blew a Marilyn Monroe JFK kiss.

A lady answered the phone, "Miller Ticket Agency."

Neil turned his attention to the female voice and inquired if he could speak to Mr. Miller about tickets he had purchased.

As she directed the call to Miller's office, Neil heard a gravelly male voice, "Miller's tickets, Miller speaking."

"Hello, Mr. Miller, I purchased four tickets for Guys and Dolls for September 14th. Since that's one month away, I was hoping I could exchange the tickets for December 15th."

Neil heard three seconds of dead air and then Miller replied in an obnoxious tone, "What the fuck do you think I'm running here? You know this isn't Macy's with some guaranteed return policy. I sell discounted tickets. You have four discounted tickets from my office. They are now yours, not mine; you can do whatever you want with them. But if you want tickets for December 15th, you will buy four more tickets. Do I make myself clear?"

Uncharacteristically, Neil meekly responded, "I realize that Mr. Miller. By the way what is your first name?"

"Phil."

"Well Phil, if I could possibly trade in these tickets, I would gladly enclose a check reflecting the difference between their face value and the actual cost.'

"Before you go any further, this isn't Let's Make A Deal. Maybe I am not making myself clear, they are your tickets."

"Mr. Miller, if we could make this arrangement, I'll guarantee I will direct a lot of business your way."

Miller screamed, "Listen Fucko, I wouldn't care if you were the heir apparent prince of Saudi Arabia, or some schmuck businessman that's going to enrich my coffers. I will not take the tickets back. So go fuck yourself and your tickets!"

Mr. Miller is going to wish this conversation had never taken place. He had crossed over a line that he would regret crossing. Neil gently placed the phone on the receiver. He didn't want to upset Noreen, so he cheerfully told her that he was going to Jackson's Steakhouse on Fordham Road to have a couple of drinks with a potential client.

Neil went to his closet to retrieve one of his finest suits, a cream-colored linen one which complimented the present New York City heatwave. As he buttoned his starched, white shirt and

Windsor knotted a flashy, multicolored tie he was deep in thought plotting out his impending plan. Fully dressed, he entered the living room to a cat call whistle from Noreen.

"Who is she? I'll scratch her eyes out!"

Neil laughed, grabbed Noreen by the waist and drew her close to his body and whispered, "Baby, you're the only one and you know it." He passionately kissed Noreen and left.

Once on the street, Neil regretted having dressed to the nines. It was hot, humid and sticky and every other adjective one could use to describe miserable. He walked at a leisurely pace to the subway and descended to the D train. A stale breeze cooled him as he walked downward on the walkway. When he arrived at trackside, the D train's door was still open as if waiting patiently for Neil's arrival. He hopped on the train and started towards the first car. This would give him direct access to the south exit of his intended destination, 47-50 Streets Rockefeller Center Station. Neil sat by a window seat which availed him the most relief from the ceiling fan directly above.

The train traveled southbound at medium speed and the repetitious soft motion of the wheels lulled Neil into a self reflective mood. Although he was a young man, his thoughts brought him back a dozen years when he was Neil the younger.

There he was once again, facing a worthy adversary and ready to do battle over some silly remark said by one of them. To this day, Neil can't even recall who said it or what was exactly said. All he knew was that he and Pat Feeley were going to have at it and have at it they did. Even though they were both pleasantly drunk, their youthful strength and reflexes were one-hundred-percent and ready to ignite.

Neil remembered Pat took the initiative with a quick right cross that missed its mark. Neil countered with a left upper cut to the stomach accompanied by a swift right hook to the face. Silent, inner rage ruled the moment. Both were punching and counter punching with half the salvos finding their mark. This went on for five minutes and their exhaustion caused an unofficial silent bell to ring.

The two combatants walked two blocks with their corner men accompanying them. Their friends encouraged them to carry on and carry on they did. Both young men, now reinvigorated by the five minute rest, continued to pummel each other. Five minutes and a respite; another five minutes and another time out. This battle approached thirty minutes with Neil having a slight edge.

It ended as Pat Feeley put his fist down and Neil doing the same three seconds later, signaling that both men had had enough. Strangely, they both put their arms around each others neck, smiled at one another, and walked away from the battle scene the only way warriors know.

They entered an arena where none of their friends would ever dare. These friends held them in awe and strangely they envied both men because they knew they didn't have the macho moxie to enter the ring that Neil and Pat had exited.

Some said Neil won the day, but he knew that no way did he win the day. It was a stone cold draw. He was so glad that he and Pat had remained such good friends. A friendship strangely reinforced by the added respect both had for each other because of a fight.

As the doors opened at Rockefeller Center Station, Neil again entered the sticky environs of the New York City transit system and slowly proceeded up the south end stairway exit. He was stunned by the bright afternoon sun which intensified the miserable weather conditions. Neil made his way south on Sixth Avenue, made a right turn onto 47th Street, and proceeded west to his eventual destination.

He opened the brass handled doors and approached the building directory. There it was: "Miller Discount Theatre Tickets, Room 303" in bold gold lettering. Neil chose to walk undetected up the exit stairs to the third floor.

He remained outside the door to compose himself before entering the front office with teeth gleaming and sporting that infectious, dimpled smile. He approached the receptionist desk and was blown away by a dark-haired Irish beauty in her early twenties. His smile was countered by another dimpled smile inquiring how she could be of assistance.

"First of all, you are the textbook definition of what a receptionist should be. Besides being beautiful, your pleasant demeanor makes the customer, such as myself, feel welcome. By the way, what's your name?"

The young girl blushed and softly responded, "Thanks for the compliments, they are appreciated. My name is Barbara Collins, what's yours?"

"Steve Zilinski. I'm a Brooklyn Polish guy that married a strawberry blonde Irish beauty. What is it with you Irish girls, are you all beautiful?"

Barbara giggled and thought to herself, why are all the good ones married? She replied, "You're going to give me a swelled head, but I must say it bolsters the ego." They both laughed as she inquired, "What can I do for you, Mr. Zilinski?"

Neil interrupted, "Please call me Steve."

"OK, Steve, how can I help you?"

Neil answered, "Well, if I was single, I'd ask you out for dinner, but seeing that I'm happily married, I'd like to speak to Mr. Miller about purchasing a twenty-five seat block of tickets. I realize he has sale agents, but I am interested in future such purchases to be used in a good will gesture on behalf of my law firm. Therefore, I want to conduct business directly with the boss."

Barbara replied, "I understand Steve, and I will ring Mr. Miller's office."

"My dear, don't bother just usher me through the door and direct me to his office. I'll take it from there. I do appreciate the attention you are giving me."

Once in the main office, Neil noticed four employees, two female, two male, all occupied and not noticing Neil's presence. As

Barbara led Neil to Phil Miller's office, she stopped and gently grasped Neil's forearm, pointing towards Mr. Miller.

"There's Mr. Miller over there by the filing cabinets. Do you want me to introduce you?"

"That won't be necessary, Barbara, I've already met Mr. Miller socially."

"OK, Steve, good luck." Barbara returned to her desk.

Neil hesitated for a few seconds, composed himself and approached Miller. Phil had his back to Neil and was busy searching through corporate files. Neil silently stood behind Miller and after a short time, Miller had that sixth sense that there was someone or something lurking behind him. He slowly turned and caught a side view glimpse of Neil Conlin aka Mr. Zilinski. His attempt at vocal recognition was short, but not so sweet.

"Who the fuck...?" and at the third word, he was decimated by a properly thrown right cross. Miller started to sliver down the five foot file cabinet as Neil was ready to uncork a left hook, but that was unnecessary. Miller was in La-La land.

As Phil made his way to the floor, Neil in a quiet staccato voice said, "Happy birthday, Fucko!" As Neil turned and started his exit, he heard the two women scream, but only for a few seconds followed by silence. Neil noticed the two ladies displaying way-to-go sly smirks, directed towards him. The two men were intensely staring at their phones as if they were expecting an extremely important call. They remained motionless as Neil opened the door to the reception area.

Strangely, Barbara didn't seem phased. Her stare showed no alarm and in a strange way may have denoted a hint admiration. Neil approached her desk.

She sarcastically inquired, "I guess the business deal didn't go so well."

Neil smiled, "Well, lovely lady, remember this: some deals you win, some deals you lose. Phil lost."

"Surprisingly, I didn't learn to punch out the person you are trying to make a deal with, in Economics 101."

"In the classroom business is taught, but in the real world, situations may drastically differ from what you may have formally learned."

Barbara laughed, "So it appears that I have to master martial arts to be a success in business."

"No," replied Neil, "but you have to realize the bad actors and deal with them accordingly. Well, Barbara, I must be leaving now. It seems like old Phil is awakening from his sleep. Here's my accountant's business card." The card showed Jack Houlihan's name. "Wait a week and give him a call. He'll be back from vacation. Tell him Steve Zilinski referred you for a position in his firm. Believe me, you'll make more money and you will be much happier than working for this sleazebag."

Neil winked at his new friend, turned around, and nonchalantly left the office and made his way to the street.

He walked several blocks, entered the subway and took the D train back to the Bronx. On the return trip, Neil was once again in deep thought. He enjoyed a giggling self satisfaction knowing that our man Phil knew why he was crumbled by one "Fucko," named Steve Zilinski. If he didn't, he would suffer the same fate in the future. Either way, Neil didn't give a shit. The D train pulled into 205th Street and Neil made haste out of the subway and back to his apartment.

As soon as he opened the door, he was attacked by three little munchkins, each one vying for his individual attention. He hugged all three, a hug that showed each how passionately their father loved them. There she was, his queen, intently observing a father's affectionate interaction with his sons. Neil eventually unfastened himself and took three quick steps, grabbing Noreen around the waist and passionately kissed her as if it was to be the last kiss. Noreen's face reddened as she was overwhelmed by Neil's passion.

"My God, that must have been a very successful business meeting. I mean, wow! You know you can make that a habit if you so desire."

Neil didn't relinquish his grasp as he kissed Noreen on the neck. He gently pushed her away at which time they both locked stares. Stares that denoted how madly in love they were with each other.

Noreen noticed a slight swelling of Neil's right hand. She inquired, "What happened to your hand, my passionate bunny kisser?"

"You know how heavy that door is at Jackson's Steakhouse? Well, I opened the door slightly and don't you know, the door closed on my hand. Once again, this proves you're right, I am the clumsiest man alive."

"I don't know what I am going to do with you. I might have to trade you in."

Neil embraced Noreen and after which he separated enough to look at Noreen's face. His heart was beating a thousand times a minute, as if it were their first kiss. His eyes welled.

He was so in love and as one tear made a track down his cheek, he whispered, "Noreen, darlin, I love you so much and never thought I could love so deeply. If I woke up one day and you weren't there, I'd be a shattered man and I'd never be made whole 'til my last breath."

Noreen responded as she stroked Neil's right cheek and brushed away the solo tear, "Listen to me Neil, there will never be another. My heart is yours and I'll never get it back."

Her cheek gently touched his and she gleefully exclaimed, "By the way, his nibs, your story about Jackson's door is pure BS, but knowing you, I'll never hear the real story."

"Well my dear, I was going to have my mother babysit these three barbarians and take you to Jim's, but now that you've uncovered the lie, we'll go to Jackson's for a steak dinner."

Then, came a final stare which resulted in a ten second laugh. Noreen pinched Neil on the cheek and turned towards the living room. She felt a soft tap on her rear end.

That night, they both dressed to the nines and had a memorable steak dinner.

Four years later, because of a dreadful disease, Neil had to leave his Noreen, but I'm sure his last words were, "I'll be waiting for you." And so from the tough streets of the Bronx came a true love story.

DANNY HOFER

6
It's Only a Game

It was midnight on Long Island and a cool summer breeze was about. All the clans had assembled, the Walshs, O'Donells, Begleys, and Lees. It was coming to the end of the yearly family gathering which had commenced at two p.m. Danny Walsh was surrounded by the male cousin contingent and all were drinking and talking sports.

Suddenly cousin Pat Walsh spouted out almost incoherently, "So you guys from the city think you are such great athletes. Why don't you bring out your softball team and humble us with your greatness."

"How the hell did the conversation switch from how great Mikey Mantle was to my neighborhood softball team?"

"So your team is so magnificent that you wouldn't consider us a worthy foe?"

"How in the world did we get to this point? I never said anything about my team or how good we were. Pat, you're letting the scotch get the better of you."

"So you are afraid that our team will give you more than you ask for."

"Jesus Christ, Pat, I don't know where this is coming from, but if you want to schedule a game, let's do it."

Slurring his words, Pat suggested we play Sunday of Labor Day Weekend.

"OK," Walsh replied, "We will be here at noon, September 2nd. I feel like this is the softball version of the Hatfield vs. McCoys. The only problem, I'm the only Hatfield." Jokingly, Walsh was making reference to the fact that the McCoy team was comprised of seven out of the nine starters being his cousins.

The next morning, Walsh woke up at Aunt Eileen's house with a hangover and a desire for greasy bacon and eggs. He sat at the kitchen table opposite cousin Pat who sported severe blood shot eyes, but he hadn't forgotten.

"I hope you're going to have enough money to pay for the keg after the game."

That was the custom, where the losers go back to the winners bar and pay for the keg of beer both teams will drink.

That statement hit Danny like a brick for he realized that most of his team would be at the Jersey shore for the holiday which would make it impossible for his team to win. Danny was dragged back to the present.

"Yeah, I can't wait to take on the big shots from the Bronx," said Pat.

Danny was about to give Pat a smack, but didn't give in to the whim. Instead, he remained peacefully silent while fiddling with his breakfast.

This solitude brought him back to the beginning of the softball season. The team had an impromptu meeting summoned by the Duke and held at The Widow's Walk. In the past, the neighborhood team never had a sponsor, but things were about to change. While the team was imbibing pitchers of beer, Duke stated that he was going to stake us to the league fee, pay for the umpires, and provide the uniforms which we must wear at each game, emphasizing the word, "MUST."

We quizzically shot glances at each other while affirming Duke's ideas, but wondering about the uniform edict. Why was he so emphatic about the uniform?

Duke revealed himself with that patented devilish smile and a slight Jackie Gleason roll of the eyeballs. Duke, without speaking implied, "Boys, you're going to love this." We all knew this was going to be a doozy and we were certainly not getting the standard uniforms for sure. Duke exclaimed, "Well men, what do you think, are we all on board?" Everyone reluctantly agreed.

Duke continued, "First, I have appointed Jim Logan as the manager of the team."

"What the hell does Logan know about anything, especially softball?" yelled Willy Dealy.

From the back of the bar Logan said, "Dealy, you're an asshole. I am the manager and what I say goes."

Uncontrollable laughter erupted.

One voice bellowed out, "Mange a team, you are going to be lucky if we let you come to the games."

The laughter went up another decibel. Duke requested silence because he knew he was losing his intended momentum.

Duke implored, like he was General Patton, "Men, our uniforms will embody the image of our manager." More groans and cat calls. "Calm down guys as I'll give you the details and origin of our uniforms."

A lone voice yells, "What details and origin, what are we wearing the declaration of independence?" asked Gordon Mc Neill.

Sarcastically, Duke said, "Funny, McNeil, ohhh, you're a funny guy."

Duke continued, "First the name of our team is Logan's Quaggas."

"What the fuck is a quagga?" shouted the gathering.

"Well boys, as you remember from your high school Latin class," groans were heard again, "a quagga is an animal whose origins are from the ass."

Quizzical faces asked for more details and that's what they got.

"Also, men, numbers on the uniforms will not be assigned."

Duke was halted with a "Why?" from the crowd.

"Because you will all have the same number."

"What the," more expletives.

"Relax boys, the universal number on your uniforms will be double zero. It will be on the front and back of the uniform. Yes, my softball-ateers, you will be acknowledging and giving deference to your manager. Yes, you will be known as Logan's Assholes."

The Quaggas were formed and Duke entered the team into a bar league.

The duplicate numbers caused opposing teams the inability to use a score book. How could you? Example, 00 pinch hitting for 00, 00 in relief for 00, in center field 00 replacing 00. You get it, frustration abounded.

Even with our whacky name and its implications, the reality was that we could play and win. At season's end, we finished in first place.

Danny came back to the present, once again to Pat's verbal barrage. Like a soft angel's breath, a gentle presence was about; it was grandma Walsh.

She spoke to her grandson, "Danny, I know you will have a fine team and sure it will be a great game, but I must say I have to pray for both teams with the situation being as it is."

That soft Tipperary brogue could diffuse any conflict.

Danny said, "Thank you Nana, at least I know there's someone sort of rooting for me."

Aunt Eileen gave Danny a loving wink and he returned it in kind. Walsh thought to himself, "Well, there was another possible ally."

It was time to go. Kissing Aunt Eileen and Nana and snarling at Pat, Walsh departed.

The Sunday of Labor Day was a beauty. It was 87 degrees and climbing with an overload of humidity. Most of the regular team was at the Jersey shore for the holiday. They were replaced by an over-the-hill gang of misfits.

Walsh approached the bar and noticed a silver-colored, medium-sized bus in front of The Walk. Danny entered the bus and smiled. It actually had air conditioning with sixteen plush seats plus a large table, a couch, and three extra seats in the rear. This had to be the doings of the one and only Mickey O, the neighborhood bookmaker.

When Walsh exited he saw Mickey dressed to the nines, black silk shirt, cream colored slacks, black patent leather shoes and sporting a beige straw fedora. Mickey always dressed like he was from Arthur Avenue, the Italian section of the Bronx. But how could this be when both parents were from Ireland? Go figure!

Walsh saw Duke and asked, "How did this bus deal go down?"

"Mickey said he'd get the bus and the driver for the whole day for two-hundred dollars. So I gave him the money and here it is."

Details of the bus rental were interesting, to say the least.

Mickey O's favorite customer, was Jimmy Smith, who owned a small fleet of buses that serviced the neighborhood schools. Jimmy was a born loser and always owed Mickey. At that time, Jimmy owed Mickey O one-thousand dollars.

Mickey O said, "Let me have your luxury bus and a driver, and I will take four hundred off the thousand you owe me."

Mickey O knew it would only be a matter of time until Jimmy would be back to owing him the original amount. The deal established had Jimmy providing for the bus and paying the driver. Mickey O charged Duke two hundred dollars and put that in his pocket.

The driver arrived and the team started to enter the bus single-file. The whole team were customers of Mickey O. He wanted to make sure his constituents were comfortable as they were studying. Studying what? The racing form. Mickey O graciously provided racing forms and made copies of all the baseball lines for the day.

The over the hill gang boarding the bus, were too old to play competitive athletics, but they weren't too old to gamble. They were a team of gambling all stars: some played horses, while others bet sports, and still others bet both horses and sports.

One member of the squad didn't gamble, but no one could deny that he was the number-one nut of the lot. His name was Artie Willis, otherwise know as, Double Drunk Artie. Why? Well, he was the superintendent of one of the neighborhood apartment houses and when he finished his morning duties, he was in The Walk tying a load on. After which, he would go home, take a nap, wake up do some more work, eat dinner, and go once again to The Widow's Walk to initiate drunk number two; hence Double Drunk Artie. You might say that's not all that crazy. Well, let's bring it up a couple of notches. Would you say that riding a motorcycle down Webster Avenue to Fordham Road and back, in the nude with your fully clothed girlfriend behind you, enough for admittance to Bellevue Hospital for the insane? Walsh knew, however, that the motorcycle event was not that unusual. There were many other escapades that established Double Drunk Artie to become the original inductee into the Nut Hall of Fame.

It was ten a.m. and off we went. Artie Willis was going to make sure we didn't stand a chance of winning. He brought a five-gallon Igloo cooler onto the bus containing three quarts of vodka combined with spicy Bloody Mary mix. Not to be undone, Mickey O topped it off with two coolers containing four cases of beer and another with just ice.

Our adventure began with the whole team drinking Bloody Mary's and studying their racing forms. Walsh figured they couldn't get that drunk because it was only to be a one and a half hour trip. Walsh was wrong. Because of the Labor Day weekend beach traffic, the Long Island Expressway was at a stand still. After one and a half hours, they were still one hour away, if lucky. They did eventually make it to the field. During the trip, half the Bloody Mary's were gone and a lot of the boys started banging down beers. The full blown team drunk was in progress and only going to get worse. As we exited the bus, our opponents and their fans hit us with a cascade of cat calls. It fell on deaf ears. The Quaggas were so bagged, they didn't take notice.

Here came the cavalcade of misfits. First off the bus was Mickey O carrying a small portable table, betting slips, and a transistor radio. He was followed by the Kiely brothers who both were union painters dressed and in their white overalls and construction boots. Next came Danny Walsh and Willy Dealy who were the only ones wearing Quagga shirts. They were also the only ones with their own baseball mitts. Mitts, that's right, Duke scrounged five other mitts for the rest of the team because none of them possessed a baseball mitt. The embarrassment of using two of the other teams gloves, just enhanced this upcoming tragedy.

Next, the Cozzi's exited. Carmine, a thirty-two year old was reasonably attired: he wore jeans, a Yankee shirt and baseball cap. He was six foot tall with a rugged handsome face and had the spring in his step, resembling that of a boxer, which he had been in his youth. His twenty-eight year old brother, George, however, brought the wow factor to a softball uniform. His six-foot-three muscular frame was outfitted with black sneakers and socks, cut off purple corduroy shorts, complemented by a black strap tee shirt with the finishing touch of wearing a purple fez hat that adorned the Italian afro he was sporting.

Next to exit, the great Artie Willis, who was to be our pitcher. His five-foot-eight frame, dark features with black greasy hair were similar to Eddie Munster. Artie wore sandals, no socks, black jeans stopping at his protruding semi pregnant belly and a white tee shirt two sizes too small exposing a quarter inch carpenter crack in the rear. Atop his head, he wore a black cowboy hat.

Then came the "Bull" Quentin Carbonara, sporting a three inch scar on his right cheek. He was 37-years old, five-foot-seven, 210 pounds, an eighteen-inch neck, and all muscle. Quentin was a brick layer whose second job was answering the phones for Mickey O on a part-time basis. He was dressed in a blue blazer, black loafers with argyle socks, tan slacks and a powder blue golf shirt, as if he was going to the track with reservations for the club house.

Now a real beauty, Johnny Walton, was half bagged before boarding the bus. He had been drinking in The Walk and asked Duke if he could play. Duke said, "Sure, you'll be our tenth man in case of an injured player." Walton continued, "Duke, I want you to know I was a major league prospect." The only problem was that Johnny is now sixty-years old and was a prospect in 1936. He exited the bus totally ossified singing, "Did your mother come from Ireland? "Cause there is something about you Irish, tell me where did you get those Irish eyes." This rendition brought smiles and applause especially from Walsh's two aunts and grandmother who were sitting in the stands.

Finally the man himself, The Duke, appeared. He wore a specially made Quagga jersey which stated "OWNER OF THE" over the lettering "LOGAN'S QUAGGAS." He had nailed a half dozen Bloody Mary's and was feeling no pain. He was waving his baseball hat to the rival fans, as if he was doing a Mickey Mantle exit from the dugout, after hitting a home run.

Finally, our beloved manager, Jimmy Logan, all five-foot-eight of him, dressed in madras shorts, white collar dress shirt, white sneakers with dress black socks and to complete the ensemble his patented fedora with green feather. He carried a large thermos of Manhattans under his arm. He began mocking and insulting the squad.

"This is a team all right, a team of assholes." Logan continued one insult after another. He did so in such a loud voice that the opposing team with Walsh's seven cousins heard every word.

To say they were bewildered is an understatement. They must have thought to themselves, "This is the Bronx bar league champions? It has to be a joke, the real team is coming in another bus." Shortly, they realized there was no other bus and this was the team. It dawned on the cousins that their team, averaging twenty-five years of age, was about to compete against a team whose average age was between thirty-five and forty, comprised of alcoholics and nut bags.

Duke realized it would be impossible to play a double header as planned. He told Walsh's cousin, Dennis that we would play one game instead. Dennis appeared to be relieved. Duke informed the umpire of the that fact and gave him an extra $20 bill to make up for the double header cancellation. He informed the ump that it could possibly be the longest game he ever will umpire. Mickey O set up his portable table while the whole team assembled single file to place their bets. Some had Bloody Mary's in hand, others preferred Budweiser. One by one, the action was vocalized.

"Mickey give me a $20 double at Belmont, the one in the first with the three in the second."

"Mickey, I'll take the Yankees laying the eight-and-a-half ten times."

"Mickey, $50 to win on the eight-horse in the seventh race at Belmont."

The bets continued, more Yankee bets, more exactas, win, and place bets at Belmont. It seemed like it would never end, but everyone got their action in. Mickey O had a big shit eating grin on his face.

Now, our owner and manager assembled the team in a football huddle and for once there was total silence. They broke from the huddle and slowly approached the third base line along side the opponents dugout. Duke was positioned at third base and Logan at home with the rest of the team in the middle. They we were bobbing and weaving, drinks in hand, facing the enemy and their fans.

Duke abruptly shouted out, as if he were Lawrence Welk with a Bronx accent, "A one, a two, and a three." The Quaggas removed their hats, or fez in George's case, and began a slurred rendition of "God Bless America." The loudest voice was Duke "Welk." While he bellowed out the standard, he was urging the fifty or so fans and team members to rise and join in. A pleasant shock wave permeated through the crowd as they scurried to stand and remove their hats singing along with the Quaggas. When the song reached its climax, Duke screamed out, "One more time folks. But this time louder and everyone singing."

"God bless America, land that I love. Stand beside her and guide her through the night with the light from above."

Duke had everyone including the umpire screaming as opposed to singing this national musical treasure. The finale had everyone cheering and applauding. It finally subsided after thirty seconds and reality set in. The Quaggas actually had to play now.

The top of the first inning commenced. First, up was Quentin Carbonara. The first pitch was a called strike. The second pitch Quentin swung at was five feet over his head. The third pitch actually hit him as he simultaneously took a swing. The ump awarded him first base.

Willy Dealy batted second. On the first pitch, he hit a hot shot to cousin James at short stop. James pivoted and threw to cousin Kevin at second. Quentin, at the same time, lost his loafer seven feet from second base. He stopped running and offered up his hands in surrender. Kevin's throw to Dennis at first, completed the double play.

Third, in the batting order was Danny Walsh, who was facing the pitcher, his cousin Pat. Pat took his mitt off and started squeezing the ball with a sneering laugh. These theatrics enraged Danny and he was ready to let it rip. The first pitch was an exaggerated change-up appearing to be on a five second trip to the plate. Danny unleashed a vicious swing which happened to be one second premature, resulting in Walsh landing on his ass. This caused an explosion of laughter from the whole team and their fans. Pat was pointing and laughing. Danny was ready to punch this bastard's lights out.

Duke's voice of encouragement was heard, "Don't let him get to you, compose yourself and let it ride."

The second pitch was launched and Danny took another fierce swing resulting in a slow grounder to Pat. Danny was running to first with Pat taunting him, "That's the best you got, Champ?" as he threw him out at first and ended the inning.

The Quaggas took the field. Artie was warming up while smoking a cigarette and drinking a Bloody Mary which he place next to the pitchers mound. Danny knew that this was going to be the longest, most excruciating and humiliating seven inning game he had ever played.

First up was cousin Peter, the centerfielder, He hit a ball past Quentin at first base and it slowly meandered into right center field. Simultaneously, George in right field and Willy in center were running at full speed and collided. George's fez flew in the air while Willy was on the ground groaning. Peter was rounding third and trotted home for a one to nothing lead. George and Willy staggered back to their positions, accompanied by Artie's insults, as he was taking a long drag of his cigarette.

Batting second was Pat's brother Kevin. Whereas, Pat was a total asshole, Kevin was one of the finest people you would ever want to meet. Artie, cigarette in mouth, threw the first pitch and Kevin launched a screaming line drive destined for Artie's head.

Artie covered up with his glove, resulting with ashes of his cigarette singeing his face. Screaming obscenities, Artie then realized that the ball had wedged in the web of his mitt for the first out.

Third man up launched a shot over the center field fence. The score was now 2-0. The next batter, cousin Dennis, drilled a shot to left for a single. Up next was Billy Calano, who was married to Walsh's cousin, Kathleen. Billy hit a grounder to Duke, who in attempted a double play, launched the ball ten feet over Carmine Cozzi's head, at second base. Brother George, minus his fez, attempted to retrieve the ball in right field. In doing so, George was able to kick the ball thirty more feet, just enough to allow Dennis and Billy to score. Now it was 4-0. Next up, Pat Walsh, received a perfect pitch from Artie and drilled a screaming line drive to left field. Danny, with a good jump, dashed in and made a spectacular diving catch. As Danny rose, he heard three cheers from the stands. His aunts and grandmother shouted, "Great play, Danny Boy!"

After the next two batters hit singles, Rick Engle hit a line drive to third and Brendan Kiely caught it.

In the top of the second, the Quaggas had two hits and a walk, but were unable to score. The bottom of the second miraculously went one, two, three.

The top of the third saw Sal Carbonara whiff for the first out. Next up was Willy Dealy, who hit a ball between left and center for a double. Danny Walsh was next. He hit another double making the score 4-1. George Cozzi, fez on and cigarette in mouth, swung at the first pitch and hit a slow, three-foot dribble down the base line. As the catcher went to make the play, George hit him with fore-arm block which sent the catcher flying into the ump. George ran at full speed to first, never losing his cigarette.

He heard a disheveled ump screaming, "Flagrant interference by the runner. He's out and he's also out of the game."

Duke rushed to the ump and in a low tone said, "You might reconsider. You see the third base coach?" as he pointed to a bobbing and weaving. sixty-year-old Johnny Walton with Budweiser in hand. "He's our only substitute."

The ump immediately reversed his decision and kept George in the game.

The Duke was next up and he hit a blooper single into right field, scoring Walsh from second. Now the score was 4-2. The Quaggas bench erupted.

They were so loud the noise drowned out Mickey O's attempt to give race results.

Above the cheers, Mickey O screamed, "Shut Up!" The team quieted and he continued on with the results of the fourth race. He shouted out, "The nine horse won and paid $11.60. The nine-one exacta paid $52.40."

A lone voice, Joe Kiely, screamed out, "That's me, I've got twenty dollars to win on the number nine and a ten-dollar-exacta on the nine-one."

Again, the home team and fans appeared startled and just could not believe how nutty the Quaggas really were.

Carmine hit a line drive to first and the top of the inning was over.

Miraculously the bottom half of the third saw no runs for the home team.

The fourth inning was to be a mood changer. The top of the inning was the usual one, two, three batters down for The Quaggas. By the bottom of the fourth, Artie and the whole team were pleasantly blasted and the last thing on their mind was playing soft ball.

The first pitch to cousin James resulted in a line shot to first, that hit Quentin Carbonara in the nuts. Cousin James zoomed past first as Artie, Carmine and Duke rushed to Quentin ignoring the ball with James rounding third and touching home plate making the score 5-2. The onslaught was in progress. Double, triple, single, one hit after another. It became so humiliating that the cousins started to bunt for hits just to rub salt into the wound.

While the hits continued, Walsh's team mates were screaming at Mickey O, "Get more beer and ice!"

Other voices from the field wanted to know who won the fifth race at Belmont while others wanted to know who was winning the Yankee game.

In between these queries, was a barrage of Logan insults. "Now you know why I call you assholes! You couldn't beat Saint Brendan's kindergarten team! Hey, Walsh, you've got such a huge family, why don't you schedule the next game against your female cousins along with your aunts and grandmother, so they can beat your ass too?"

The hits kept coming and there were the cousins laughing and taunting. The one who was enjoying it most was good ole cousin Pat. Walsh thought to himself, "Man, I would love to kick the bastard's ass." That thought was interrupted by the third out and the score at 10-2.

The top of the fifth was uneventful as the Quaggas were dispatched one, two, three. The bottom of the fifth saw a disinterested Quagga team. As a matter of fact, they didn't give two shits about the game. From the field, guys were screaming at Mickey O that the beer was warm. Mickey O responded that he had sent the bus driver for two more cases of beer and four bags of ice.

Quentin Carbonara was screaming from the field, "Who won the sixth race? I've got thirty to win on the eight horse."

Other voices wanted to know what the score of the Yankee game was. They cared about the Yankee score, but they sure as hell didn't care about the score of the softball game.

Artie was still pitching, but his dungarees were inching dangerously low exposing a bit more of the carpenter crack. He was poised on the mound still smoking accompanied by a can of Bud by his feet. His drunken condition caused him to walk one batter after another. After four walks and with the score 11-3, Artie decided to have a conference at the mound with the catcher, Joe Kiely. The meeting lasted thirty seconds, during which the rest of the team were shouting obscenities as the ump rushed out to the mound to get the game started again. His gesture was for naught for the entire Quagga team started to leave the field.

Duke took charge and implored the men to go back to their positions. The team agreed when Duke said he was coming in to relieve Artie. Artie couldn't be replaced because their tenth man, Johnny Walton, was passed out in a borrowed beach chair, unconsciously fulfilling his third base coaching duties. Artie gave the ball to Duke and staggered toward shortstop. Duke pitched decently, but he still gave up two more runs making the score 13-2.

Walsh ran over to his grandmother and aunts to apologize for the foul language. They waved him off and said they had heard worse. When Walsh returned to the bench, the team was laughing and joking. The beer had finally arrived packed in ice. Walsh thought to himself, "Losing 13-2, humiliation, and embarrassment doesn't even phase these lunatics, but warm beer leads to a potential uprising."

The top of the sixth was as quick as usual. One, two, three and the Quaggas were on defense again. Duke immediately got Billy Calano and cousin Dennis to both fly out to center field. The next three batters got three hits scoring two runs making the score 15-2. With a man on third, Duke walked the next two batters loading up the bases. The next occurrence verified that blue collar proverb, "Just remember when things are bad, they can always get worse." Now we had good guy, cousin Kevin, at bat. He swings at the first pitch, hitting a spinning ball one foot from home plate.

Joe Kiely leapt from his catching crouch and grabbed the
ball firmly in his right hand. Instead of tapping home plate with his
foot for the third out, he rifles the ball to his brother Brendan at
third base for what he believed would be a force out and the end of
the inning. The ball sailed by Brendan ten feet high and wide of
third base.

Walsh sped in from left, went horizontal to the right, as the
ball flew fifteen feet to his left. This play could only be
accomplished by a drunk, cross-eyed fielder which was a reality. As
Danny hit the outfield grass, a solo weed caught onto his Quagga
jersey and forced its way up past his stomach, past his chest, and
covered Walsh's head. The bases cleared and the score was now 19-
2.

Danny attempted to stand. In the ten seconds that he was
blinded by the jersey and was attempting to remove it from his
fully covered head, laughter erupted all around him. His team
laughed their nuts off and the entire contingent of the opponents
and their fans were hysterical.

Pat Walsh pointed, laughed, and taunted Danny as he
entered the batter's box with two outs in the sixth. Duke's first
pitch was a called strike. The next, another strike with Pat taking a
vicious cut. The third pitch, right down the middle with
diminished speed, was right in Pat's wheel house. He connected
and away it went, high and deep into left field. Walsh sped back to
the left field fence. Danny was suddenly blinded by the sun as the
ball made its rapid decent. He totally lost sight of the ball, and then

sadly, the ball hit him on top of his scull and careened over the fence for a home run.

Laughter again, as if it were a Vaudeville show with back to back comedy acts. His team, the other team and fans were hysterical once again. Big mouth Pat laughed, pointed, and taunted again; even more demonstrative this time.

Danny was so enraged it resulted with him sprinting in from left field screaming, "I'm going to kick your fucking ass."

But, there in his way was Duke and he whispered, "Don't let this dipshit get the best of you. Calmly walk back to left field and let's get one more out."

Duke prevailed and Walsh with his head down in shame, slowly returned to his position. 20-2 it couldn't get any worse. Well it didn't; the next batter took three nonchalant swings, not even attempting to make contact, and the dark inning was finalized.

The top of the seventh saw three Quaggas up and down with nine swings and the game was complete.

The celebration commenced, jubilation, laughter and hugging. No, it wasn't the cousins celebrating for they were in shock after experiencing this farcical athletic display. It was the Quaggas celebrating. The horror was over and the beer was cold. There was still a couple of races at Belmont to be bet and best of all, the Yankees were winning in the top the eighth.

As both teams lined up in single file to shake hands, the Quaggas were staggering and giggling. Duke was first, followed by Logan mocking the Quaggas with every step. The Cozzi brothers were carrying Johnny Walton who could no longer walk. Next the Kiely brothers, convinced that they made the correct play pertaining to the third base grand slam debacle. The rest followed, amusingly chatting away, and at the end was the "Bull" Quentin Carbonara, sporting dark sunglasses which made him look like a Mafia hit man.

The cousins sheepishly acknowledged the nice game hand shakes and if an observer, who hadn't seen the game, would think they were the losing team. Even big-mouth Pat was quieted. After these post game salutations, it was off to the cousin's bar, The Pink Lady to enjoy the losing teams obligation of buying a keg of beer.

Danny Walsh, before leaving, walked over to his grandmother and aunts once more. Again, he started with an apology, this time for his actions and language towards the end of the game.

Walsh said, "Grandma, I'm so embarrassed that you saw all these wacky shenanigans today. I cant't imagine what you must think of me and my friends."

His grandmother responded, "Ah Jesus, Danny, remember this was only a game. The most important thing in life is the real game, and the real game is family.

"I will tell you this boy, when Grandpa Walsh and I married that was the beginning of our loving family, with your two aunts, your father and Uncle Pat. We had difficulties, but love saw us through and as a result I have sixteen grandchildren and a few great grandchildren. God has blessed me with this legacy. There is, however, one secret I have kept till this moment."

Inquisitively, Walsh asked, "Really Grandma, what is it? That is if you want to tell me." Grandma Walsh was silent for an elongated five seconds. She lovingly smiled at her daughters and with a slight glisten in her eye, she turned toward Danny.

"You know Danny Boy, you're the only one that doesn't live with the clan in Long Island. You are certainly quite a flamboyant, mischievous lad, but I know your heart is a loving one. Here is the secret my sweet. When I get up each morning, I kneel to say my daily prayers. The first person I think of is my Danny Boy. I wonder how he is faring in that far away land they call, The Bronx. I wonder if he realizes how much I love and miss him and how his family has him woven into the Walsh fabric. I asked the Lord to let you know that there is an empty spot in my heart reserved for you and no other. Yes, it is that particular spot that aches when you're not present, but my whole heart is overwhelmed with joy when you appear."

Danny was shocked and temporarily overwhelmed with a joyful sadness. To think that this emotion could emanate from the matriarch of his family and that this person would love him to that degree brought a trickle of tears from both eyes. Grandma and his aunts encompassed him in a group bear hug with his aunts brushing the tears away.

As Grandma released her grip, she stated the obvious once more, "Remember lad, what happened today was only a game. Now my boy, you truly know what the real game is."

They all kissed once more and Walsh departed and made his way back to the team.

He saw Duke talking to his cousin, Dennis. and giving him a camera. With no one else left on the field except Dennis and the Quaggas, the team wanted to get onto the bus. Duke hushed their boisterous discontentment stating that a team picture must be taken. All of them, in grumbling agreement submitted to Duke's wishes. Logan, of course, was bemused by the fact that there should ever be a photo of these losing assholes.

He stated, "Don't any of you have any shame?" Shaking his head as he sucked down his eighth Manhattan. He yelled at Duke, "Ok, let's get it over with, assholes."

Duke arranged the shot, with the entire team in the stands behind a stewed Logan, sitting in Mickey O's chair. Duke, whispered in Dennis' ear his final directorial instruction, after which he took his place in the stands immediately behind Logan.

Dennis was methodical, he directed the exact position of the team and insisted that Jimmy stop fidgeting and look directly into the camera. This lasted for five minutes and Logan now directed his wrath to the entire Walsh family. Logan staring at Dennis remarked, "Danny, I'm sorry I called you a stupid asshole, you can't help it, your whole family is a bunch of dummies."

The click was heard, but Dennis with a wry smile implored everyone to remain still for one more shot, in case the first one didn't come out right.

Logan screamed, "What an asshole," as the second shot was snapped. Everyone dispersed and entered the bus.

It was a short trip to the Pink Lady. Within thirty minutes everyone was off the bus and positioned comfortably at the bar. Sir Duke, the generous, came through once more. He ordered two six-foot, Italian heroes, two trays of baked ziti and meatballs, and a few trays of macaroni and potato salad. It was enough to feed both teams and more. His largess didn't stop there. Besides the keg, he paid for a two-hour open bar.

One thing could be said of these Long Island relations, "If it's free, it's for me!" There were shots of all types of liquor being inhaled at break neck speed. MikeyO brought out four decks of cards and proceeded to the back room of the Pink Lady. We were far from being the toughest neighborhood in The Bronx, but no one could deny our supremacy at drinking and gambling. Our decimating loss was a distant memory, but our immediate revenge was now unfolding. Walsh's cousins, with the unleashing of free shots and beer were taking their intended affect. They were slurring their words so badly that their intended insults towards the Quaggas backfired making them look like babbling buffoons.

Mickey O gathered the home team into the back room and introduced them to Mickey O Blackjack. The rules were simple, you were paid two to one for blackjack and five-card-Charlies, a hand with five cards under twenty-one. The immense advantage for the dealer was that the player would lose when he tied the dealer. Compare this to casino blackjack where a tie would be a push, meaning that the player would get his bet back.

Mickey, the shrewd business man that he was, stated that anyone who's dealt a blackjack could take the deal, but with one caveat. The stakes were between two and thirty dollars and with six players being seated at the table, the new dealer would have to have at least $180 to accommodate the possibility of six maximum bets. Another angle to Mickey's plan was if he forfeited the deal, he would just limit his bets to two dollars until he was dealt a blackjack and reclaim the deal.

Duke arrived with a tray of shots which the cousins inhaled before the blackjack action commenced. Duke partnered up with Mickey O on this caper and was just oiling up the machine before a withdrawal from the Royal Bank of Walsh. After two more trips with shots, Pat Walsh and the rest of the ensemble were whacked and even if they wanted the deal, they were physically incapable of dealing out the cards. This gave Mickey O full reign as the dealer and he slowly removed all their US currency.

With the Duke happy hour over and the keg near its end, the Quaggas began to assemble in the front of the bar. Mickey O, after retrieving the cards, was counting stacks of various denominations as he left the table. The Walsh clan and friends were laid out throughout the bar and blackjack area. They were drunk to the nth degree with the six blackjack players relieved of all their money.

With their imminent departure, Danny Walsh diagnosed the entire day and came to this conclusion. The Quaggas lost the softball battle, but his grandmother was right, it was only a game. When Walsh saw the mental and physical destruction of his extended family, it gave him a perverted sense of enjoyment. He saw Mickey O and Duke dividing their gambling proceeds. Not only was the Mickey O and Duke partnership a success, but a number of our degenerate gamblers unleashed their prowess at seven card stud. Two stud games went on in the same back room as the blackjack game. The result saw the Kiely brothers, the Cozzi brothers and Quentin the Bull unleashing poker hell on any dipshit that wanted to indulge. The Bronx boys cleaned them out.

The Quaggas in the beginning of the day were humiliated, but it didn't phase them, no bitching, no crying, just a continuation of that Bronx insanity. An insanity, that involved those gentle immoralities they embraced each day of their blue collar existence. No denying it, they acted like the true assholes they were at the Pink Lady. But they were assholes who drank like professionals and with Johnny Walton unconscious on the bus they actually all appeared sober.

Mentally Walsh tenderly embraced his crew. He was so proud of them and concluded that if he had the choice of his beginnings again, be it Park Avenue, Riverdale, Scarsdale, or any other prosperous neighborhood, he would once again choose the

Saint Brendan's boundaries with all its deprivations and hard core life lessons learned. These basic experiences prepared all the young boys of the neighborhood to take on life's journey and all its ups and downs.

Walsh was brought back to reality. He saw Duke quietly directing the gang, minus Logan, to make haste and board the bus. Danny knew that Logan was about to be had. After Duke ushered all of us out, he went back to The Pink Lady and told Logan, "Hurry up! The bus is about to depart." Logan, at the far end of the bar, started berating Duke for not telling him sooner because he just ordered another drink. With that said, Logan chugged his drink down on the way out.

The bus was filled, less Logan, and parked outside the bar which was next to Connor's super market. The stream of patrons entering and exiting Connor's was to be the desired component for Duke's next Logan-erization. Duke was seated to the right of the bus driver, who was given a ten spot to follow Duke's specific commands.

The premise of Duke's premeditated evil was simple. The bus' front door would remain open until Logan was ten feet away. The driver would close the door and slowly drive in a large circular trek around Connor's parking lot with Logan chasing. It was magnificently simple, but would result in maximum Logan mayhem. A mayhem that would produce a scarlet-red face and "assholes" spewed in abundance, like fireflies on a balmy summer night. Logan's exit from the bar was distant enough for the first maneuver. This resulted in a few low-voiced, mumbling "assholes." The bus stopped in front of Connor's with the front door open. Logan, in a slow sprint, approached and again the door closed and the bus went twenty feet further beginning its intended circular pattern. It was now full blown Logan, screaming obscenities, as people were exiting and entering Connor's.

Duke's inventive trip continued around the parking lot drawing the attention of a diverse crowd, which included grandmothers, nuns, young couples with children as all of them commented and pointed at Logan. Twenty minutes later, Duke granted mercy and after fifteen door closings, the door finally remained open and in entered an unhinged Logan. He was swearing at everyone from the bus driver to Johnny Walton, who was still passed out.

The bus ride home was hilarious with ball busting galore.

Logan yelled sporadically, "You're all assholes and all of you suck at softball."

The last of these insults came as we were approaching the neighborhood.

Logan stood up and screamed out, "Assholes, as of this moment, I resign from my managerial position." It was so proper, as if he were addressing British Parliament.

Duke jumped up from his seat and made this, "Give me liberty or give me death," pose. He affirmatively pointed to this bus load of mad men and said, "I refuse Logan's resignation and besiege all Quaggas to do the same." In this setting, Duke bellowed out, "All those who refuse Logan's resignation, raise your right hand and state, I."

The entire drunk cartel less Walton, raised their right hand and screamed, "I."

Duke faced Logan and said, "The Quagga organization refuses your resignation and I, as the owner, extend your managerial contract one more year."

Logan, with a bewildered look said, "So I keep a position where I drink watered down Manhattans and watch you dipshits get destroyed."

Duke replied, "You got it Jimmy, how lucky are you?"

The bus finally arrived at The Walk. One by one, the boys meandered off the bus; the last were the Cozzi brothers, carrying Walton who was semi-conscious.

The bus driver knew none of the Quaggas before the day began. He displayed a dismay that revealed, "What the fuck just happened today?" When he would reach his golden years and had his grandchildren surrounding him to hear stories of his younger years, he would definitely recall this infamous softball team. He would tell them of the bus ride itself and reveal the insanity he observed at the game, the bar, the incident in the parking lot with Logan. The astonished look on these teenage faces would be somewhat diminished by the final "But" by grandpa. He would tell them that if he would be involved in the same scenario, he would pay them to be their bus driver. He continued to say, Duke and company would refuse such a proposition and would enhance that days wage four fold, the same as what actually happened. His pocket would be stuffed with money supplied by Duke, Mickey O, and the team collection taken at the end of the trip. He would reinforce the notion that this group was truly insane with a quirky humor that would rival any Abbott and Costello sitcom.

He would reminisce how much they sincerely cared for each other and their loyalty to one another had no bounds. He would acknowledge their love of neighborhood and their blue collar morals. They embraced their heritage, one where a handshake was a deal, no written contract necessary. A heritage where even though you would probably get your ass kicked, you would still stand your ground. A heritage where there was no elitism, no person was better than the other. They wouldn't trade that in for any higher social status. The one thing they had over the country club, filet mignon eating type, was that they lived in a world of reality. A world of extreme highs and lows. They celebrated each others successes and bolstered one another through tough times when only the fidelity of a friend could help them though. Then grandpa would end his tale by telling the grandchildren that the men of The Widow's Walk were the real deal and without them, America would not be as great as it is.

DANNY HOFER

7
The Unveiling

The bus ride was now a memory and the football season was in its third week. For Monday Night Football, The Widow's Walk always served hot dogs and discounted pitchers of beer. This Monday was different because Duke had upgraded hot dogs to hamburgers. Previously, Duke had informed his clientele the reason for the upgrade was to celebrate a portrait unveiling at halftime. He informed them that the unveiling would be written into neighborhood folklore. Most of the Monday night lunatics asked each other, "What the fuck is an unveiling?" No one cared because tonight they would be feasting on hamburgers.

Logan arrived just before kickoff.

He approached Duke and said, "I heard there is an unveiling at halftime, is that when you are finally going to reveal that you are the high, exalted, mystic ruler and king of all assholes?"

Duke grinned shyly and replied, "You know Jimmy, even though you are a bird brain, you almost guessed it."

"You're an asshole, buy me a Manhattan."

Duke obliged and they lovingly busted each others balls while they observed a packed bar inhaling burgers prepared by Artie Willis and Johnny Walton.

The two minute warning had arrived. The burgers had been consumed, beer drinking was in overdrive, and Logan was just finishing his third Manhattan. The seconds ticked down to halftime while Duke cleared a booth area in the middle of the bar. The purpose was to allow all patrons to gaze unhindered on the object to be unveiled. It was securely hidden by a purple cloth the size of a large bath towel.

The first half ended. Duke stood up on the booth's bench and assumed his orators' position. Walsh was with the Cozzi brothers and Greg Cassidy at the end of the bar. Directly in front of the covered surprise was the usual crew of all stars and Logan.

Duke began his speech to an unusually quiet crowd. The patrons anticipated an event that would never be forgotten and they wanted to relish every word that Duke was going to say. First, the Duke thanked all the members of the Quaggas softball team.

Logan interrupted, "Team, what team? It's a team alright, a team of assholes."

Cat calls bellowed throughout the bar causing Logan to shut up.

The Duke continued, "As you can see, this is a portrait. It is not patriotic in nature. It will not overwhelm the observer with emotion. It's not pretty nor is it ugly. Once you lay your eyes on it, it will be so profound that you will relay tonights unveiling to future generations."

128

Everyone was scratching their heads over what Duke had just said. He asked Logan to stand on the other side of the booth to help remove the drape. Duke told Jimmy to remove it very slowly.

Logan responded the usual, "You're an asshole."

The unveiling was completed and the crowd was stunned for a moment. The laughter started low and crescendoed to a roar that could be heard two blocks away. There it was, cousin Dennis's enlarged photo. It revealed Logan seated in front of the Quagga team with cross bats in his hands and Johnny Walton to his immediate left was passed out on the ground. Unbeknownst to Logan, the entire Quagga team were shown with their pants down and their asses waving at the camera. Under the enlarged photo was a bronze plaque stating, "Who is the real asshole?"

Logan returned to the bar floor and chuckled, "Duke, you did it again, asshole."

Duke smiled back. He ordered the patrons to the end of the bar and instructed them to come to him one at a time. All the patrons declared Logan to be the real asshole. Logan was the last person on line and Duke asked again, "Who's the winner?"

Logan gave Duke a sheepish grin and quietly answered, "Me."

Duke stood on the booth once again. "All votes have been cast and the unanimous winner is one James Logan."

Everyone raised their discounted beers towards Logan and toasted, "To the real asshole, Jimmy Logan, the king of all assholes."

Laughter erupted again and a voice proclaimed, "Here's to King James!"

After ten seconds, the crowd had settled down and Duke addressed them again. He stated, in a serious manner, that there would be one more toast.

He reverently declared, "The vast majority of us had served in the Armed Forces because of love of country. Today, there are young men that are not here because of military service, be it Vietnam, Korea, Germany or other places throughout the world. They defend our country and neighborhoods. Let's pray that they return to us safely."

Duke instructed Walsh to play a song from the juke box and said, "Raise your glasses once more to salute our men serving and raise your voices in song."

Kate Smith began her famous rendition of "God Bless America." The voices began in a soft melodic tone and as the song progressed the voices became louder. One could also hear a few tear choked notes or two.

Over in a darkened corner of the bar was Logan, singing the song in such a low tone, it could barely be heard. He stood there at attention with a single tear slowly moving down his cheek. He was thinking of WWII in the Pacific. A place where he earned two purple hearts and bronze star with valor. He thought of his brothers in arms and those who never returned.

The song had ended and Logan's melancholy mood was interrupted by Duke's voice. "Get over here, Jimmy, I am going to buy you a Manhattan."

Logan smiled, "It's about time, asshole."

Duke replied, "You're welcome, oh great king."

As they both laughed, Duke told Logan that he was treating him to a steak dinner the next night. Duke knew his friend quite well and knew why Logan was sheepishly hiding in the corner. He was aware of what Logan experienced in the war. Duke realized that his friend was far from being a dummy. To the contrary, he was quite intelligent and Duke understood that. Logan had risen to Detective first grade in the NYPD and solved many cases using his innate intelligence and bulldog persistence. Logan was the real deal, but Duke never acknowledged it because that would erode the basis for Logan humor. As they both stood at the bar, busting each others balls, Duke gently put his arm around his shoulder and gave him a hug.

Logan snapped, "What the hell are you doing?"

"I wanted to let you know that you are my main man."

Logan's suspicious response was, "This is why you're an asshole."

They both smiled knowing they had an unbreakable bond that would be that way for years to come. The portrait incident was used by Duke to be a tutorial. This silly occurrence evolved into a patriotic theme that signified sacrifice and love of country and reminded everyone at the bar what a privilege it was to be born in the USA. That was The Duke and that was the neighborhood.

8
A Somber Birthday

It was nine a.m. on a beautiful spring morning and the posse of five were finishing their coffee and tea at The Widow's Walk. Today, there would be no laughter, Duke and the boys were departing on a journey they wished they didn't have to take. Their journey would end at St. Vincent's Hospital located in lower Manhattan. The boys were going to see their friend for probably the last time.

Neil Conlin was battling, but losing his fight against cancer. Neil served his country in the Marine Corps and graduated from Fordham University. After which, he joined the NYPD and at the same time attended law school at night. After several years, Neil passed the bar, resigned from the Police Department and set up a law practice. He was one of Duke's best friends and they became partners in The Widow's Walk.

Neil was the epitome of a man's man. His word and hand shake were all that was necessary to cement a deal. When you needed a tough street fighter, he was your man. He never backed down from any physical confrontation and you would be betting on the wrong side if you thought he would be the loser. His kindness and humor were always evident and all who knew him understood that this human side was not a sign of weakness, but a compassionate love shown to his friends.

Neil's family was the light of his being. He and his wife, Noreen, had five sons all under the age of eight. Noreen was a woman extraordinaire who was the loving light Neil needed to pursue his life's goal.

Duke Callahan was driving, Danny Walsh was in the front, Ray Quigley and Willy Dealy were in the rear with Jimmy Logan crammed in between the two. The car, a two door Mustang, lacked the room needed for four large men and a diminutive lunatic, but away they sped. There was an uncomfortable silence during the ride, sprinkled with short low voiced conversations about inane topics. All of them were most likely self indulged in their memories of Neil and how he had enriched their lives by just being a friend.

Danny Walsh remembered those nights, when early in a shift at The Widow's Walk, he and Neil would be able to converse. Neil would always pump Walsh up by showing admiration for his educational pursuit. For Danny Walsh, like Neil Conlin, was attempting to become the first college graduate from both sides of his family. These conversations reinforced Walsh's drive to succeed. Danny viewed Neil's sage advice, wisdom, and gentle prodding as if it had come from an older brother's concern for the younger.

Walsh's heart was overcome by a depressed malaise as the car was parked and they entered St. Vincent's. When they arrived at Neil's room, they hesitated entering because they couldn't accept what they were about to see. Quietly, which is quite unusual for this bunch, they approached Neil's bedside. There he was smiling and consoling each one of us for he intuitively knew our hearts ached. Neil, once more, thinking of his buddies was determined to lift this veil of sadness. The visit turned 180 degrees evolving into a comedic event with ball busting lines flying around as if they were ping pong balls at a Saint Brendan's Bingo.

The hour visit seemed to last only thirty seconds. The doctor and two nurses entered, signaling that our time with Neil was at an end. We looked at each other seeking support, but knew we each had to say goodbye in our own way. One by one, each man grabbed Neil's hand to shake it, but the shake turned into a soft hug. In unison, the group in a low chant, said, "Take care, Neil," as they left. They left the room single file, each man holding back the sniffling one would hear from a pre-kindergarten child.

Encountering the bright sunshine of the day, they left the hospital with watery eyes. They filed into Duke's car to their assigned seats with Logan squashed between Ray and Willy. The uneasy silence lasted for a few moments. At a light on Third Avenue where Duke made a left to go northbound, he uttered the words which would diminish the sadness encompassing the car.

"Let's get some lunch and a couple of cocktails."

Danny knew a caper was about to unfold that had already been arranged by the Duke. As usual, he knew nothing of the what, when, and why. It was a mystery just the way Duke liked it. Keep 'em guessing. That was the comedic genius of Duke Callahan. At the conclusion of all his escapades there was always one-hundred-percent, gut-wrenching laughter.

The journey north continued and Logan, in an unusual respectful manner, brought Duke's attention to a bar on the west side of Third Avenue by 19th Street.

"Robert, there's a gin mill, pull over." Logan now referring to Duke by his actual name as opposed to "asshole."

That was it, hook, line and sinker. Duke has snagged his prey.

He replied, "Jimmy, I can't park there, it's a bus stop."

At 25th street on the east side of Third Avenue, Logan said, "There's a bar and restaurant, we can get a highball."

"Sorry Jimmy, there's garbage truck parked in front."

"You're an asshole, park in front of it."

"It's too late Jimmy, there's too much traffic behind me."

Logan's face reddening one more shade, said, "What the fuck does traffic behind you have to do with parking, you're an asshole."

They arrived at 49th Street and shining in their faces was a neon sign, "McGuire's Chophouse."

Logan pointed out, "This is a great restaurant, pull in front of it."

Duke slowed down to a speed which allowed another car to take the spot in front of the restaurant. Duke had to maneuver around another parked car to return to the flow of traffic. Duke took both his hands off the wheel and shrugged his shoulders suggesting there was nothing he could do about the traffic.

Logan snapped, "Where the fuck did you get your license? In a Cracker Jack box?"

Logan was past irritated. It was similar to a Cape Canaveral launch; the initial blastoff was in progress. All in the car were snickering, not exactly laughing, but on the verge.

It was at 68th Street, after excuses for passing three more bars, that the second rocket, the one that sends you into orbit, was ignited.

Logan spoke again two levels above conversational, "Asshole, make a left here, we'll go to Hell's Kitchen where my buddy owns a bar and grill."

Duke purposely refused to make the left stating that it was illegal to make a left hand turn onto 68th Street.

Logan, leapt from his cramped quarters screaming into Duke's ear, "There's no sign stating no left turn," as Duke passed 68th Street continuing north. Jimmy had lost it. It was alcoholic insanity.

Quigley and Dealy were laughing uncontrollably. The laughter resulted in Logan being squeezed tighter between the two, so secondary, "assholes," were hurled at them. Logan's face was crimson on the verge of purple, signaling that it could possibly be emergency room time for him.

His voice increased one more octave, "Where the fuck are we going to eat asshole?"

At 82nd Street, that Duke parked the Mustang in front of his favorite Manhattan steakhouse, The Red Coat Inn. Walsh got out of the passenger seat, enabling the guys in the back to exit. Logan elbowed Dealy in the neck insuring that he was going to be first out. As he stepped on the pavement, he hit Danny with a NY Ranger style body check, which set Walsh back a few steps. With a burst of speed, similar to a wide receiver, Logan darted into the restaurant. Once in the restaurant, he encountered a lovely Irish born waitress as he sat down.

"What will it be, lovey?" asked the young girl.

Logan tersely responded, "Give me two Fleischmann Manhattans."

When the boys entered, they saw Logan inhaling his first Manhattan. As the boys set down, they ordered their first round which included Logan's third Manhattan. The one liners were coming from every which way and most of them ending at Logan's door step. The restaurant was half full. The Widow's Walk crew were drinking, eating, and laughing, but still thinking of Neil.

The mood was broken by the voice of another Irish waitress who inquired, "Hey boys, another round or some dessert?" as she affectionately pinched Logan's cheek and at the same time continued, "How about some sweets for you lover boy?"

The table howled as Logan blushed because of a woman being present, there was the absence of a deluge of, "asshole," from Logan. Danny peered at the Duke and there it was, that look, the look that signaled something mischievous was about to occur.

Walsh's mind started to ruminate, "What will it be?" All that he knew was that Logan was to be the recipient of whatever occurred.

After the drinks were delivered, the two waitresses were approaching our table with an elaborate birthday cake. They started singing the happy birthday chorus and slowly ourselves and everyone else, customers, bar tender, and manager, were blasting out the tune. And when it got to the name recognition, Duke, with almost a banshee like scream sang, "Dear Jimmy." Duke lead the crowd in a second rendition of the tune, but at a louder pitch. Everyone was giving Logan their sincere birthday sentiments. The song ended with a thunderous applause as the two ladies kissed Logan on both his cheeks.

Walsh thought to himself, there's the Duke showing his sappy side.

Danny extended his hand and offered a heartfelt, "Happy birthday Jimmy."

"You know you are a bigger asshole than that asshole."

Danny saw Duke's devilish smile and knew that he had also been had.

Logan continues, "It's not my birthday, you asshole. This asshole," pointing at Duke, "orders me a birthday cake every time we go to a different restaurant, making sure everyone sings happy birthday."

Walsh was mystified because he could not understand how the Duke could create such comedic situations from the craziest of scenarios.

DANNY HOFER

9
Bye, Bye Birthday

Six months after The Red Coat Inn birthday incident, Duke, Logan and six other wackos were taking their seats in a new steak house in The Bronx.

After being seated, Logan suddenly stood up and turned in Duke's direction, "Asshole, no birthday cakes! I mean it!"

Duke sincerely acknowledged Logan's request and emphatically reaffirmed absolutely no birthday cake. The dinner progressed with merriment and language decorum for there were a couple of large families with kids surrounding the crew.

As they were having after dinner drinks, the waiting staff was entering with a birthday cake beginning their rendition of happy birthday.

Instantly, Logan leaped from his seat screaming at Duke, "I told you. No more birthday cakes. You asshole."

An innocent blue-eyed, five-year-old boy said to his father, "Daddy, it's that man's birthday too!"

Daddy, a six-foot-two brute of a man, gently said to his son, "I don't think so."

After which, the father glared at our table, because Logan's reaction put quite a damper on his son's fifth birthday. The other people at the family table weren't very amused. Two men seated at the table were exactly the same size as the father. One was the boy's grandfather and the other being the father's brother, dressed in his Marine Corps uniform sporting many medals and a combat tan from Vietnam. Also present were two aunts and the boy's mother and grandmother. All four ladies were scowling and appeared ready to lead the charge from their table to Duke's with the intent of beating the shit out of Logan and anyone else who would come to his defense.

Duke rose to the occasion and scurried over to their table. Quickly, he offered his apology to the whole family. He implored that they all have an after dinner drink on him and asked permission that our table to be able to join in another rendition of happy birthday to the birthday boy. Duke inquired what the young fellows name was and learned it was Kevin.

Duke whispered something in the waiters ear after which happy birthday was loudly sung. Upon completion, Duke gave Kevin a twenty-dollar bill and the young boy thanked him profusely.

Duke said, "Kevin, you don't want to eat cake." He turned the boy towards the waiter and there it was, a gigantic ice cream sundae with hot fudge syrup and whipped cream.

Duke gently touched the boys face and whispered, "Happy birthday, Kevin."

Kevin, gave Duke a hug, and with a beaming angelic face whispered back, "Thank you so much."

Once again Duke used his ingenious personality to bring everyone together either for the humor or the good. Duke was the first to organize charity events to help a family or a cause. Personally, he gave whatever he could to a friend in need, be it money or a job. Duke's random acts of kindness were always a secret between Duke and recipient. He always said to Walsh, "Remember Danny, a favor or act of charity should always be a forgotten memory." Meaning, that it should be done, with no strings attached or accolades received.

Duke had done it again, he left a family smiling and toasting our table. To this day, Walsh believed that if you put Duke in a situation under the right circumstances, he could prevent a world war. Duke picked up our bill along with the family's drinks. You see, in Duke's mind, that's The Bronx way.

DANNY HOFER

10
The F Word

It was early October and football season was in full swing. The men both old and young were happy. It was the time of year when a majority of their sports betting took place. Betting football was a religion and our guys were amongst the most pious parishioners. It was a delightful Tuesday night with temperatures in the low sixties and no humidity. This night eventually brought a peaceful, cross-ventilation sleep across the neighborhood. These were the nights most people anticipated, where you saw your neighbors strolling the streets enjoying the balmy weather. Walsh's crew would stroll to The Widow's Walk and indulge in a few brews with their other favorite bartender, Tom Flaherty.

Tom Flaherty was not Jimmy Logan. He showed you respect and expected the same. He was the philosopher bartender who instructed the young, drinking gamblers how to conduct themselves while in his presence. When ladies entered The Walk, all foul language ceased and a code of respect was enforced by Tom. Chivalry was alive and well as women sat at the bar and the men were all standing. That was the Flaherty way. In casinos they refer to the biggest gamblers as "whales." Well Tom was our whale. He bet on everything sports and horses had to offer. Tom never welched on a bet and taught all of us neophytes to follow the same credo. Flaherty taught us how to drink.

"Don't be a nuisance, don't be a loud mouth and don't start fights."

At sixty, Tom was still a menacing figure. He was six-foot-one, 240 pounds, and sported a mane of pure white hair, a ruggedly handsome face, and a nose that informed the observer that he was a boxer in his youth. Many tales of his boxing prowess had become neighborhood legend.

On this Tuesday night, Walsh, Dealy, Cassidy, and the Cozzi brothers were discussing an event that confirmed all the tales about Tom.

Jimmy Feeley, younger brother of Pat, compared what occurred last night to the historic sailor story. The comparison of the two incidences copy catted each other.

Moose Morano bought Walsh and the boys another round of drinks and Feeley started to spin the tale of the prior night.

Last night was Monday night football. Discount beers and free hotdogs meant the bar was full with many of the neighborhood characters present, Mickey O, Quentin Carbonara, the Cozzi brothers, and most of the members of the softball team.

Halftime arrived and four guys known to the neighborhood came through the door. They were not regular patrons of The Widow's Walk. One of the four ordered one beer from Flaherty, after which the four commenced to inhale several hot dogs.

Duke noticed this blatant maneuver and approached the group and said, "Only people who were drinking could have any of the food. One beer for four guys doesn't cut it."

Immediately, one guy whacked Duke in the mush and that proved to be a serious mistake. Flaherty tippy toed from behind the bar and built up a deadly head of steam that finalized with his right fist crushing the face of Duke's assailant. One of the other young men took a feminine swipe at Tom. He was met by a left hook and right cross which opened his nose like an uncontrollable river of red. He landed bleeding and unconscious in the booth under the infamous "Who's the real asshole?" Logan portrait. One of the four had exited as soon as he saw Flaherty's fury. The last guy was bum rushed out the door by the Duke. Feeley opened the door as the guy was airmailed into the night air. Duke and Flaherty dragged the unconscious foe from the bar floor and together they shot putted him out the bar with his head colliding with a parked car.

The instigator was the only one left, which delighted Flaherty. Flaherty took his two Irish mitts and placed one around the neck and the other pulling his foes hair. The dazed victim was dragged and half skip-walked to the bar's exit. Flaherty motioned Feeley to open the door again. Tom launched his right fist with the speed and accuracy of a guided missile and made perfect contact with the teeth of the original instigator. His exit had the semblance of a drunken ballerina pirouetting out to the street with two small white chiclets exiting his mouth.

The skirmish took no longer than five minutes, but the aftereffects took on neighborhood folk lore. A tale that confirmed once again, don't mess with Tom Flaherty.

Feeley ended the tale of the previous night as the unusual silence engulfed the five some.

The silence was broken by Gilroy as he stated, "Well, Feeley your common sense prevailed. You opened the door for Tom, because if you would have tended to the wounded, God knows what would have resulted. You might have taken a trip to the emergency room courtesy of one of Flaherty's thunderous blows."

Laughter erupted.

After another round of drinks, Walsh told the Tom Flaherty and the sailors story, as relayed to him by Duke Callahan.

This incident occurred fifteen years prior at McCauley's Bar & Grill, the most popular neighborhood saloon. Tom, in his mid-forties, was bartending at McCauley's. It was early Saturday night in the middle of a summer heat wave and the darkness of night had not yet arrived.

With the brightness of the setting sun, the door opened and three uniformed sailors entered and assumed their positions at the bar. Tom acknowledged their presence and continued his conversation with two ladies in their late fifties, who frequented the bar from five to eight p.m. every Saturday. They were Flaherty groupies who adored Tom and he returned their loving attention in a caring, chivalrous manner. Mrs. O'Brien and Mrs. Lynch were drinking their Manhattans professionally made by Tom.

The three sailors were impatient and wanted service loudly voicing their displeasure. Tom slowly turned from the ladies and told the sailors to relax as he inquired what they wanted to drink.

One of the sailors abruptly replied, "Three beers."

Tom delivered the beers and continued his conversation with his two female admirers.

It was obvious that this was not the first bar the three sailors had been drinking in. Their slurred voices grew louder and they began to use the F word quite often. This was verboten in Flaherty's world, especially as his two favorite lassies were enjoying their drinks listening to the Tommy Dorsey band playing on the juke box. Tom quickly approached the sailors and in a calm tone said he respected their service to our country, but foul language would not be tolerated while women were at the bar.

Tom poured three more beers and said, "Thanks for your service, these beers are on the house."

He meandered towards the opposite end of the bar to serve Duke Callahan and crew another round of drinks. He bemused them with a short amusing quip and then turned and walked toward Mrs. O'Brien and Mrs. Lynch at the other end of the bar. As he past the sailors, he heard the F word and other blue language that could easily be heard by the ladies. Tom repeated his first warning with a little more teeth, emphatically stating, "No more foul language."

Tom continued entertaining the ladies; their attention intensified with every word that he spoke. The ladies were pleasantly resigned to the fact that others may have Sinatra, Como, and Elvis as heart throbs. They didn't care; their 'wow' man was big Tom Flaherty.

A boisterous "Fuck!" came from the sailors, prompting Tom to turn from the ladies and walk slowly towards the young men.

With his crimson face, he stated, "How many times have I got to tell you guys about cursing?"

The loudest of the three made a critical error. An error that would be life changing, because til the day of his death, he'd wish that he could have taken back these loud, slow cadenced words.

"Fuck you, fat boy."

Instantly, Tom's eyes bulged out of his head. He didn't say a word, he didn't have to, his face spoke volumes He turned slowly from the three sailors and patiently removed his white apron. Sporting a gentle smile and a wink, he asked the ladies to excuse him as he lifted the wooden bar arm and exited the bar service area.

It was a mere twenty-pace walk to the three. The first five steps took on a speed and cadence of one talking a pleasant stroll through the Bronx Botanical Gardens. Steps six to fifteen slowly increased in speed. Steps sixteen to twenty turned Tom into the eighteen-year-old, amateur, light-heavyweight champion he once was.

The loudmouth quipped, "What the fuck are you going to do, fatty."

That was step twenty. Tom now on his toes, pivoted towards big mouth and hit him with a left hook. The sailor was starting to melt when he was the beneficiary of a right cross that instantly rendered him unconscious. As the other two took flight, Tom sprinted behind them and was able to grab the slower of the two. He turned him around and blasted him with another beautifully executed right cross that saw sailor number two take flight and go head first through one of the meticulously designed stained glass windows. Flaherty exited McCauley's and attempted to chase down number three. He knew instantly that he could never catch him and gave up the pursuit. When he entered the bar, he dragged the first sailor to the exit and gave him the old heave-ho.

Entering once again, Flaherty observed Tom Gilroy tending to the second sailor who was bleeding profusely from the nose with superficial cuts on his left cheek, a result of his collision course with the stained glass window.

Flaherty was furious, "What are you doing Gilroy? Get away from this asshole or I will put you next to him."

Then Tom lifted sailor number two, and had Gilroy open the entrance door, and gave the sailor a blast that launched him into the street next to his mangled buddy. The whole ordeal lasted no longer than five minutes, but the mayhem was undeniable.

Tom, trembling slightly, took his place behind the bar next to his two lady friends.

Mrs. O'Brien was the first to voice her concern, with that unique, sweet, melodic accent. "Tommy, darlin, surely we don't want to see a young, handsome man like you have a heart attack."

Mrs. Lynch echoed the same sentiment and further stated she would pray for him tomorrow at Mass, and ask the Lord to erase the stress and guilt Tom might have incurred from the incident. Amazingly, these two lovely ladies totally ignored the mental and physical state of the sailors as their main concern was for their beloved Tom. Tom, graciously acknowledged their well intended concerns, but as he headed to the other end of the bar, Flaherty took on a somber demeanor. He paused at mid bar to reflect on what he had just done.

Even though these three lads were totally in the wrong, they were still wearing the uniform signifying these sailors were defenders of freedom for USA. Tom, being a World War II veteran, had never struct a man wearing the uniform. He let his temper get the better of him and now a wave of guilt encompassed him.

He slowly approached Duke and his crew. These guys were all newly minted veterans discharged a year prior. Duke and company had always been looked upon Tom as a surrogate father and Tom was aware of this. He wondered if a bit of his luster had been diminished because of this violent outburst.

His usual silence was noticed and Pat Feeley asked, "What's the matter, Tom? You're not feeling bad about what happened? They deserved it and you obliged them."

Pat's words of support did not diminish Tom's gnawing sense of guilt. Tom signaled Gilroy to meet him at the rear of the bar next to the kitchen. When they met, Tom said he was sorry for being so nasty to Gilroy and that he would never punch his lights out. Gilroy exhaled a sigh of relief, knowing he was not going to be the next victim of Tom's notorious right cross.

Flaherty continued, "Gilly, come with me to the kitchen, we'll get some hot water, soap and clean bar cloths to take care of these sailors."

The bar was half full. The patrons attentively observed Flaherty and Gilroy and were unanimously wondering, what the hell was going on as both men exited the bar.

Both sailors were nursing their wounds, still in a semiconscious state. They would have screeched in horror, but their faces were so swollen, they couldn't voice their fear. They both saw Tom with what appeared to be a pot of boiling water.

They both had the same thought, "What's this fat fuck going to do now, scald our faces?"

In abject fear they clinched each other, knowing that they would both be going to sick bay for quite a long time, undergoing face reconstructive surgery. Tears of fear streamed down their faces. There wasn't anything they could do, it was inevitable, disfigurement was awaiting them.

Tom bent down and placed the pot of water and soap on the curb next to the sailors. Flaherty said ten words that would never be forgotten by our wayward cursers. "I am sorry that I did this to you boys."

Tom continued as Gilroy cleaned their faces with soothing warm water and soap.

"You now know that you do not use foul language when women are present? Right?"

"Yes, sir!" the two twenty year olds replied in unison.

After using multiple bar rags, the cleansing process was completed. Now these men of the sea looked half normal. However, the remnants of the assault, the swollen blackening parts of their faces, could not be scrubbed away. Flaherty and Gilroy lifted the two to their feet and slowly walked them back to the bar. A nauseous feeling overtook the two.

"Could it be, could it possibly be, we are being marched into this strange bar for a second ass kicking?"

This was quickly erased from their minds, as the smiling face of Duke urged them to join the crew for a drink courtesy of the neighborhood.

Flaherty interrupted and stated, "They'll have their drinks after they apologize to the ladies."

The sailors went to the other end of the bar and sheepishly offered their apologies.

Mrs. Lynch quipped, "Ah, the two of you are fine lads and isn't it a fact, we all make mistakes. Sure, that's why we have confession. It is a shame you had to pay such a price for your transgressions, but I truly believed you both learned a lesson."

The boys were speechless for a few moments.

Until one sailor stated, "Ma'am, we definitely learned a lesson."

Both sailors moved their eyes fearfully towards Tom.

Mrs. O'Brien, noticed this, "Ah, boys, you don't have to fear Tom, he is our lovable teddy bear and he will not be hurting the two of you again."

The sailors looked at each other in astonishment, "Lovable teddy bear?"

The women instantly started laughing, with the sailors joining in, but their laughs stung due to their blackening facial bruises.

Hearing this group laughter, Tom approached the four new friends, having heard something about a teddy bear. He turned towards the ladies with an inquiring look and motioned his hands in a, "What's this all about gesture?"

Mrs. O'Brien addressed his dismay, "Tom, darlin', we were just saying that the boys unfortunately saw the wrong side of our Tom. Sure he is really nothing, but a big teddy bear."

Laughter again, but the two sailors owned the laugh of the nervous one in an octave much lower than the first guffaw.

Flaherty gave off a muffled chuckle. His instantly transformed to a face with furrowed eyebrows, and two piercing eyes zeroed in on our villains. The stare was only five seconds, but to the sailors it seemed like five excruciating minutes. Flaherty's short stare caused the two sailors to become pale with beads of sweat forming at the hair line and dripping down their foreheads. The uncomfortable silence was broken with Flaherty unleashing a big Irish smile and a chuckling wink to his girlfriends. He quickly motioned the two in the direction of the Duke crew where drinks were waiting for them.

He looked at the girls once again. They were both making haste and ready to start their short trek home. As Mrs. Lynch left her bar stool, she motioned Tom to come closer.

Softly she whispered, "We want to let you know, we are in the Tom Flaherty fan club."

When the two ladies made their retreat, they pinched Tom on both cheeks. Tom blushed crimson and gave an, "Aw shucks," motion with his hands.

The ladies were about to exit as Mrs. Lynch gently blew a kiss to Tom saying, "Goodnight sweetie, we'll see you next week."

The guys all knew that in a strange way, a gritty blue collar existence had commandments that must be adhered to. They were not commandments formalized by organized religion, but commandments they were. The times these commandments were violated, the perpetrator must be forcefully shown the error of his ways. Why? The answer, simply put, is so he would never violate the neighborhood code of conduct again. It was a guarantee for the violator for life and that was good.

That was not to say that there could also be a nonviolent remedy and in some situations that may have been the best alternative. However, when the invisible line established in the blue collar world had been flagrantly crossed, the Flaherty way, sadly, was the only way. If the morality clause is violated, that cannot be tolerated.

Tom Flaherty was the mentor necessary to usher a young boy into manhood. He was the arbiter of what was right or wrong. Tom was the truth serum and when properly administered, it was undeniably the right path for living an existence based on the highest moral qualities.

DANNY HOFER

11
The Stiletto

It was hot, muggy Thursday morning in July when Danny Walsh was awakened by his mother's voice, "Wake up, Danny, time to go to work. While you're in the shower, I'll be making breakfast."

"Thanks, Mom."

Walsh had lost his prior job of being a truck driver for Ralph Ward, a regular in The Widow's Walk. Ralph owned a heating and air conditioning firm. Presently, his business was in a decline forcing many layoffs, including Danny.

Ralph loved Danny as if he were his only son. Ward was a man not to be taken lightly. He survived the Depression. He was a fighter pilot in WWII. After returning home he was a laborer in construction for several years, while he attended trade school at night. Eventually, he was accepted into the sheetmetal union as an apprentice, where he learned everything there was to know about the instillation and maintenance of large commercial projects. When he became a mechanic, he took an interest in the other side of the comfort equation. That was steamfitting, which was the instillation and maintenance of the heating systems for commercial and residential construction. Years passed and Ralph decided to start his own air conditioning and heating corporation which became very successful. He had made the right connections along the way and the projects came rolling in. Presently, the industry was in a downturn and many projects slowly dried up. Ralph had to lay off almost half of his working force and Walsh was one of the casualties.

Ralph Ward reached out to his friend Buster Reilly and asked if he could possibly hire Danny Walsh. Buster worked for Haas Heating & Air Conditioning, a company which flourished because of their permanent contract status with the New York City Board of Education. Buster agreed to hire Danny with the status of working on permit and not as a member of the steamfitters union. This temporary hiring condition was allowed by the union because of the abundance of work and not enough schooled union steamfitters. While heating and air conditioning work diminished for Ralph, it thrived throughout the metropolitan area with no shortage of work for the unions and their workers.

So there was his nibs, taking a shower and pondering the reality of having the mother of all hangovers twenty-four-hours later, on Friday morning. As he exited the tiny bathroom, his senses were titillated by the smell of coffee, bacon, and eggs. Mae responded, "Eat it all, you will need your energy for a hard days work."

Walsh silently chuckled, little did Mommy darlin' know, that it was a stomach lining needed for the debauchery that awaited him in an hour's time. Work was not on the agenda. It was payday which meant early morning cocktails. This would last til three-thirty at which time, Buster Reilly would dismiss his crew of misfit steamfitters, fully bagged up on whiskey and beer.

Kissing his mom, he exited the apartment and found himself encountering the makings of a scorching hot and humid day. It was already 7:50 a.m. which forced Walsh to double time his way to The Widow's Walk. Danny was dressed in his powder-blue, long-sleeve shirt, dungarees, and construction boots. All standard fare for a steamfitter.

Walsh was in front of The Widow's Walk on time. Opening the door, he was met with a blast of morning air conditioning that dried the sweat that had started to form on his forehead.

Another blast, the verbal kind, "Good morning, asshole," which brought Walsh's attention to the diminutive, pea-headed James Logan, smiling like a Cheshire cat.

Walsh thought, "Oh, boy, this is going to be some day."

As was to be expected, Logan stepped up the rhetoric. "Hey dipshit, go join the rest of your steamfitting assholes. Tell Reilly, Mr. Asshole, that the only steam you dickheads create is the steam that comes out of his ass."

Pounding the bar four or five times, Logan breaks out into uncontrollable laughter. It always amazed Walsh, how Logan entertained himself with no one else laughing, but him.

Buster and his crew of seven disregarded Logan's antics and ordered a round of Budweiser to start the day. Buster and Artie Willis proceeded to the kitchen area to retrieve four chess sets and boards.

It was the time of the great chess battle between Bobby Fischer and Boris Spassky for the World Championship. This continuing spectacle trickled down the US social strata and came to a stop with blue collar workers. It was a contagion which formulated into an obsession with chess.

With a bewildered look, Logan foisted a short staccato laugh aimed directly at Buster. "Reilly, are you kidding? You were left back four times in grammar school. You have to have a brain to play that game. If you put all eight of you together, maybe, just maybe, you'd come up with one brain."

Willis interrupted, "Well, you have to have some smarts to become a great basketball player and Buster was all city in grammar school."

Logan shot back, "Yeah, he was a six-foot-one, 180 pounds with a full beard, sixteen-year-old playing against twelve-year-olds. Like I said, Artie, the genius Reilly was left back four times. It would have been more, but the principal just wanted to get rid of Einstein. Yeah! If this moron is the brains of the outfit, I ask you, is there one fully developed brain among the eight of you?"

Laughing uncontrollably, Logan gags out, "I rest my case."

The insults had stopped and the chess boards were placed in The Walk's largest booth which accommodated all eight men comfortably. Sheepishly, Buster went to the bar to order another round. Logan took it out of the fifteen-dollar-a-man pool which was enough for drinks and a variety of hero sandwiches.

Logan chuckled, "Another round for the whiz kids?"

Buster playfully retorted, "You know if you keep this up, it might reflect on your tip."

Logan snapped back, "My tip! If I had to survive on tips from you and your knuckleheads, I'd have to beg for mercy from Saint Brendan's to give my family food and shelter. We'd end up in the basement of the Church. To make things worse, I'd have to hear a line of bullshit from the Monsignor and a whole lot of nuns about my intake of booze."

Logan's look turned sombre and he spoke to Buster while filling the tray with beer. "Hey, Buster, maybe you could help me if the Logan family fell on hard times. You know, speak to the sisters."

He stared into Buster's eyes and in a slow, rising voice, "Do you know why I am asking you to be my go between, if the future becomes bleak? I'll tell you why, because you were the only dimwit in Saint Brendan's school history who was left back four times. Which means, you know all the penguins seeing that you did thirteen years including Kindergarten. By the way, the nuns still don't know how you graduated Kindergarten on time. Be that as it may, all that time you spent in grammar school, you know each one of them on a personal basis and therefore you will be my front man."

Buster's eyes locked into Logan's and they stared for a short while. Then both burst into laughter. Logan gave Buster a reassuring, you'll always be alright with me wink. Buster grinned and made his way back to the booth.

One had to realize that Buster was the alpha-male till it was quitting time. He designated the four sets of rivals for the early morning chess matches. Off they went into the land of kings, queens, bishops, knights, rooks, and pawns. They all knew the basic concepts and move directions of each piece, but controversy still prevailed.

"You can't move your pawn in any direction!' Willis proclaimed.

Bobby Gilroy answered, "Fuck you! You move that fucking bitch Queen of yours any way you want."

"Idiot, that's the rules. Certain pieces have limitations on their movement. The Queen has no limitations."

Gilroy answered, "What's with the big fucking words, limitations? I gotta be word shamed by an asshole who was thrown out of Cardinal Hayes and ended up in Dewitt Clinton, otherwise know as, Our Lady of the Reservoir."

Willis shot back, "Listen, shit head, at least I graduated high school."

Gilroy shyly responded, "Well, I would have graduated, but in my junior year I got into a jam. The judge said jail or the marines. I opted for the latter."

The chess banter continued for the majority of the morning.

"Shithead this," and "dummy that," coupled with "moron" and "dipshit" created verbal carnage.

By eleven with a six pack in each of the eight, the "Fuck Chess!" wing of the steamfitters chess club prevailed. So by round number seven, chess turned into checkers. But the cursing and berating didn't ceased.

This vile atmosphere persisted until Gus Geary blurted out, "Fuck Checkers!"

It was almost noon which signaled the end of all mental pursuits. Now drinking along with ball busting was the order of the day. Moose Morano went next door to Frank's Deli and brought back the hero sandwiches as the bagged-up crew devoured their lunch like it was their last meal.

After lunch, Buster signaled Logan to dispense a round of Cutty Sark shots, his favorite scotch. On the signal of their leader, all eight consumed the first of many shots. In 1972, it was only 50 cents for a nip of beer and 75 cents for a shot. Since the customer was getting a buy back after paying for three drinks, the boys had plenty of money left to continue on the road to annihilation. All of them could drink three times more than the average person. This was a result of starting to drink at thirteen or fourteen years of age. By the time they were legal, they all had developed an unhealthy tolerance for alcohol. In other words, "They all could drink!"

The afternoon clock ticked away and the bar started to fill up with patrons. This increased the smoke from Marlboros and Camels which enveloped the customers into a mystical haze. In the 1970's, ninety percent of The Walk's drinkers inhaled one to two packs a day. The "Fuck it. You're gonna die of something anyway." attitude reinforced their compulsive smoking and therefore no one cared.

Freedom arrived at three-thirty when half of Buster's crew departed and escaped further damage to their livers. Buster remained along with stalwarts Danny Walsh, Gus Geary and George Cozzi. The remaining four were about to reach the point of no return when they ordered beer number twelve and their fourth shot of scotch.

The crowd increased and Logan had all the bar stools occupied by construction workers, off-duty police officers, and postal workers. You name the occupation, it was represented. They all systematically had their three beers or drinks, along with the complementary fourth round. After which it was home to the family.

This was not the case with these steamfitters. Their day's conversation, up to now had gone from chess to politics to which female film star had the nicest set of tits. As the clock struck five, there was only one topic and that was gambling. All four of these lunatics were active horse players. If it moved, no matter what it was, they'd bet on it.

Gus Geary, Danny Walsh, and George Cozzi started betting trotters at Yonkers Raceway when they were fifteen-years old. They would find some means of transportation to the track: sneaking onto the rear exit of a bus, hitch hiking, or getting a ride from the older guys in the neighborhood. Once at Yonkers, they would stealthy climb a fifteen-foot fence with six-inches of barbed wire on the top. Presto! They were in the clubhouse of Yonkers Raceway.

166

Gus had the look of a twenty-year old which enabled him to take care of placing all the bets.

That system continued for a while until they all matured. Now, all three were in their mid-twenties and had yet to slow down so the inevitable, "Off to Yonkers" verse was chanted.

Plans were made to leave The Widow's Walk at six p.m. so they wouldn't miss the daily double. Buster said he would take the company van and Cozzi and Geary agreed. Walsh declined opting to take his own car.

Danny intended to leave after the fifth race. His plan was to get lucky at a new singles bar that had opened north of 233rd Street and White Plains Road. If he had taken a close look in the mirror, he would have seen one slobbering drunk, not exactly dressed to the nines. The reality of the situation was, he had absolutely no chance of success in his romantic quest.

The Yonkers four began to exit The Walk, leaving a nice tip for Logan. Buster made a mistake.

He told Logan, "Jim, that's for you."

Logan responded so quickly as if he knew Buster was going to utter those words, "Well, assholes, thank you. It's just the amount I would expect from four losers. You know you and the other three beauties couldn't handicap which priest would say the noon Mass on Sunday. Remembering back in the day, there was an old Italian guy, Patsy Peaches who would go through the neighborhood selling fruit from his wagon pulled by a horse. This horse had to be the oldest horse in the world. Those horses, Buster, are the type of horses you and your asshole buddies bet on, hence you are all born losers. But wait a minute, if you assholes could bet on the horse that would finish last, you'd all be millionaires." Logan spewed out his patented, devilish laugh and in an un-Logan manner said, "Hey assholes, thank you for the tip. I hope you break the track."

He shot the boys an impish smile along with a wink.

As he left the bar, Walsh scratched his head in amazement on how complex a human this lunatic Logan was. You never knew if he was with you or against you, but when it was all said and done, he always seemed to come out on your side. Yes, the father of all assholes, really cared for us and would do whatever he could to help a friend.

The four departed and encountered a blinding setting sun accompanied by ninety-percent humidity and a sweltering ninety-degree temperature. Walsh had Bertha, his '65 Buick Skylark parked in front of The Walk. What a gem this car was! Bertha had sun bleached peeling silver paint with an ever growing crack on the front windshield and a variety of dents that gave the appearance of being hit by rock size hailstones. Danny loved this car. He thought of it as a whacked out specie of an auto, akin to a mechanical version of himself. Sure, it had many faults, but it kept on running. Walsh and Gus Geary took Bertha to Yonkers.

Twenty-five minutes later they had parked and with racing forms in hand they went to the clubhouse. They met Cozzi and Reilly in the upstairs bar who were able to commandeer two more chairs, which allowed all four to be comfortably situated. The boys studied their racing forms. It was amazing. After consuming well over a dozen beers and a half dozen shots of booze, they were standing straight, clear-eyed and conversing in a sober tone. The crew ponied up another drinking pool.

Their favorite track bartender, Charlie Maloney, shouted out salutations and asked what they were drinking. "Four beers," was the reply. The boys loved Charlie because he was a clone of them. He was a drinking gambler. The crew and all the other bar patrons called him by his nickname, Yogi. One would ask why as he didn't look like or have any of the quirky characteristics of one, Yogi Berra. Charlie was diminutive in size, five-foot-seven, 140 pounds, wavy black hair, clear blue eyes that revealed his emotions. Sad or happy, you could read Charlie like a book.

Charlie would go to the tip jar before every race, and he would ask one of his clientele to make a wager for him. The only problem was that Charlie had a very tough bar manager who was strictly by the book. In other words, he was a dickhead. If the manager saw him cheering and snapping his fingers as if he was a jockey with a whip, these actions would indicate that he was betting instead of giving his full attention to the bar. As stated previously, this manager was one son of a bitch. He took pleasure in firing anyone: servers, bus boys, and especially bartenders. Charlie truly loved his job and didn't want to lose it, so he invented the Yogi system. His rating as a bartender was A plus, but that could not be said about his gambling prowess. Unlike Logan, he made the patrons, each and every one of them, feel like they were special. He'd cheer each bettor with his patented, "Knock 'em dead." He sincerely cared for us because he was one of us. Maloney and Logan were exact opposites, but deep down, they loved us and rooted for us. With Logan, you had to dig deep to realize that, but not so with the gracious manner of Charlie Maloney. Walsh chuckled to himself thinking of the both of them, but especially Yogi.

During the running of each race, Charlie disappeared from view and assumed his patented catcher's position. Once in position, he would scream for his horse with his fingers rapidly snapping. After each race, he'd reemerge to the standing position. Walsh watched this elaborate procedure many a time and it wasn't only the catcher's position part that was unique. Charlie had a lookout at each end of the bar and if either saw the manager he would yell, "Batter up!" This was a signal for Charlie to stand up with a bottle of vodka in his hand, as if he had just retrieved a replacement bottle from the well. The manager siting rarely occurred, but when it did, the Yogi system prevailed.

It was five minutes till the start of the first race. After all four had done their required studying, the group conversation took place. As usual, each one tried to convince the other three that his horse would win. Cozzi was preaching the #3 horse driven by William Houghton. He hooked the #3 horse with the #1 horse in the second race for his daily double bet. Buster was more of a sports bettor, so he just hooked up two drivers he liked in the first two races. He really didn't need a form to study, he just picked drivers.

Gus Geary was a stone trotter and sports bettor. The day he left the womb, he had determined his life's pursuit. Should I be a teacher, doctor, or lawyer? No, to all of them. I will become a degenerate gambler. Gus was single and would remain so because of his love of gambling. He knew he was a rover and his independent nature eliminated the possibility of the settled life with a wife and kids. He was no schmuck, he took on gambling as a serious pursuit. Geary studied intensely, whether it was the necessary sports statistics or the accumulation of large stacks of racing forms to compare the past performances of the present nights horses.

Once, as a compliment, Walsh told Geary, "You know Gus, of all the gamblers in the neighborhood, you're probably the best. You actually might be a small winner or the very least, a break even bettor. That, my friend, is true."

Gus humbly replied, "Thanks, Dan, I know you mean it and I appreciate the compliment."

Walsh had never quelled the habit of betting trotters from his early teens to the present. It was his gambling passion. Although he bet sports, the half-mile oval was his true wagering love. Walsh was more than a decent handicapper. He watched each race intently and made notes of any horse who had a difficult trip. Especially, if the horse was boxed in on the rail and had the ability to maneuver off the inside and make a strong finish. Walsh took notice even though the horse might not finish in the top three. Along with evidence from the racing program that the horse had previous rail problems, would be enough for Walsh. Even though he was in his mid-twenties, Walsh had many years of experience with the trotters. Over time, he developed the discipline of not betting all races, only those that fit his criteria. Some nights, he would only bet two, other nights five races, but never the whole card.

This particular night, he loved the #1 horse, Blackie Adios. Walsh had seen Blackie Adios's last two races in which the horse had two bad trips. Danny determined that the driver had screwed up, but tonight Del Linz was his replacement. Linz was a top driver and the horse was dropping in class. This did not go unnoticed and the bettors made him second favorite at 5 to 2 odds. Despite the reduced odds Walsh still loved Blackie Adios.

He conferred with Gus Geary and his response was joy to Walsh's betting heart. Gus loved Blackie Adios. Buster and Cozzi had different picks which Walsh dismissed. Danny bet $20 to win and a $10 daily double hooking Blackie Adios and the #5 horse in the second race. Geary's daily double wager was Blackie Adios and the #4 horse in the second race. Charlie overheard the two talking and told Walsh to put $4 to win on Blackie Adios. Charlie also wanted two $2 doubles, Blackie Adios with #4 and #5 in the second race.

The call announced before each race sounded, "The Marshall calls the pacers." One by one, the trotter pulled sulkies approached the starting gate. The gigantic car driven gate, with all the horses in place and behind, started its increasing speed around the far turn and into the stretch. Twenty yards before the finish line, the gate sped away and the horses were off. Maloney assumed his Yogi position as if he was asking for a fast ball down the middle.

As he clicked his fingers, he was yelling, "Come on, Blackie Adios! Come on Blackie Adios!"

As the horses passed the stands for the first time, Blackie was in the second row placed behind the lead horse. Walsh was happy. Blackie Adios was not going to be boxed in at the rail this time. Linz was giving him a good ride.

Charlie was verbally involved, "Come on, Blackie! Come on!"

His fingers assumed the imitation whip cadence. As he approached the back stretch, Linz had his horse in perfect position, still second behind the leader in the second row. Around the far turn the horses from the rear were making their moves on the leaders. The leading horse in the first row, closest to the rail, seemed to be reenergized and was attempting to pull away and steal the race in the home stretch. Linz seemed to have a sixth sense. Without looking, he knew that horses were gaining from the rear. So as Blackie approached the top of the stretch, Linz swung out three wide.

Charlie Maloney was screaming, "Come on, Blackie!"

His two hands were percolating, as they took on the sound of castanets during a Carmen Miranda Latin dance.

Maloney implored Del Linz, "C'mon, you fuck! Don't hold him back!"

Walsh and Geary both knew it was evident that Blackie Adios was going to win. Three seconds later, Linz pulled ahead of the lead horse and won by two lengths. Danny and Gus put their arms around each others shoulders, congratulating themselves. At the same time, Charlie appeared like a jack-in-the-box with a big Irish grin. Even though, it was only a $4 bet on a horse that paid $7.60, Charlie was ecstatic. He didn't care how much he won, it was just the fact the his horse finished first. That was the ultimate gambling high when it came to trotters.

The boys ordered another round of beers with shots of Cutty Sark. The scotch ignited the start of a second drunk. Just when they thought they would cool it and just sip a few beers, the scotch fired through their veins. This prompted Walsh to beckon Yogi and request another round of scotch. This time it was five shots because Yogi was included. The conversation level climbed a few levels and the ball busting was on the rise.

Barbs, like, "How the hell could you bet that horse?"

"You're a born loser. You're better off taking your gambling money and putting it in the poor box at Saint Brendan's."

"You know it takes some brains to bet horses. I guess yours is on vacation. Oh, excuse me, they're always on vacation."

After each insult, the four of them laughed as if they were being heralded. It was amazing, the worse the insult, the louder they laughed.

All of a sudden, it was as if a cone of silence enveloped them for there was only seven minutes left till the second race. They had to prepare their strategy for the upcoming race.

At three minutes to post time, Walsh proclaimed, as he pointed to Buster and Cozzi, "Listen you knuckle heads, cover whatever insane bets you make with a 4-5 exacta box. Those are the two horses Gus and I like and for once you'll have a shot at winning."

Both insulted men stared at Walsh, as if they were offended. The two dummies fostered a sly smile while nodding in agreement.

They both shrugged and Cozzi stated, "What the fuck do we have to lose. Even these two assholes could be right."

If Cozzi's and Buster's bets go down, Walsh's bet might bail them out. Now all four were in agreement. Two minutes to post and they all made their way to the betting windows.

In their haste, Walsh shouted to Charlie Maloney, "Hey, Yogi, I'm putting a bet in for you."

Charlie gave Danny the thumbs up with a wink.

They returned to the bar, tickets in hand, hearing that famous call again, "The Marshall calls the pacers." Walsh's horse, the #5, was 10 to 1. Gus's horse, the #4, was 6 to 1.

Walsh had Maloney's $2, 4-5 exacta box and snapped at Charlie, "That's coming off your tip at the end of the night."

Charlie softly chuckled as he was about to assume his position. Buster and George were more concerned with their bets on the #3 and #7 horses, but they also had a $2 exacta box 4-5 saver.

Gus's #4 horse dropped in odds to 5 to 1 while Walsh's #5 horse went up to 12 to 1 as the horses lined up and were moving with the gate. When the gate sped away, the horses were in full stride. The usual two line took precedent with five horses single file on the rail and five horses single file on the outside with both lines snugged together. They remained that way until their first time past the finish line.

Charlie, in his position, was unusually quiet: no voice, no fingers. That changed when the #5 horse from the rear of the second line, made a monster three wide move at the near turn adjacent to the clubhouse. The hinges came off.

Charlie skipped vocal one and hit the pinnacle vocal five with both fingers cracking. "Come on five horse! Get your ass going!"

Charlie, noticed that the #4 horse was boxed in at the rail, as they approached the back stretch. Maloney sounded as if a hot poker was shoved up his ass. He was screeching like a devil-possessed banshee and his voice carried throughout the clubhouse dining area. The #4 horse driver was Eddie Robb.

Charlie continued, "C'mon, you fucking #4 horse! Get off the rail! Eddie Robb, you've always been a piece of shit! Now redeem yourself!"

Walsh was rooting for his horse and cracking up at Maloney's antics at the same time. The two lines started separating at the far turn which enabled the #4 horse to escape from the rail. Eddie Robb, was known to be one of the most crooked drivers, although in actuality, they were all a bit shady. He took the #4 horse three wide into the top of the stretch. There was only one horse to beat, the #5 horse with a five length lead.

The stretch run was intense. We were all cheering and Charlie knew he had a lock on the exacta.

His voice however was still blaring, "Don't break! Don't fucking break!" He was referring to the case where some pacers break stride during the race, and that eliminates them from winning.

In mid-stretch, the #4 makes an amazing move and gains rapidly on the #5. With the finish line a mere ten yards away, the #4 is dead even with the #5 and ultimately wins the race by a half length.

Bedlam breaks out. Charlie leapt up as if he was on a trampoline.

His face was red with delight. "Danny Boy, thanks for thinking of me."

Walsh responded, "Charlie, my man, if you're happy, I'm happy."

And a happy Walsh he was. He didn't have the $2 exacta box. No! He had a $10 exacta straight, #4-#5 because he wanted insurance to protect his daily double.

Charlie slipped another round of scotch to the boys, "Courtesy of Yonkers Raceway," and he didn't leave himself out.

As they hoisted and toasted with five shots, the second race was deemed official. The exacta paid a whopping, $116. They all had it once, including Gus. Walsh had it five times and his buddy Gus had the daily double five times, which paid $50. It was a nice payday for all, but Walsh profited the most.

Over the next couple of races, they gave some of their winnings back, but they were still comfortably ahead. The fifth race brought them back to even on their winnings. They each bet $20 to win on a horse that Gus loved. The horse won and paid $6.80 that prompted another round of beer and scotch for the boys.

The second drunk was now full blown. The needling, back slapping, and laughter increased a notch. They were loving every moment. They were neighborhood; therefore, they were brothers. They all had each others backs. When the siren sounded distress for any one of them, it was all hands on deck.

Walsh was feeling no pain for the second time that day, but the day's activities slowed him down a bit. It was time for him to leave. He told the boys he was going to a singles bar on White Plains Road called, The Lyons' Den.

Departing he felt woozy and a bit slow of foot. His walk was in a zig-zag pattern, instead of a sober, straight line. He was stewed to the gills. No matter what, Walsh felt amorous and was determined to hook up with some raven haired, voluptuous beauty.

The problem was verbal communication. His speech pattern was a cross between slurring and incoherent babbling. He failed to realize that as soon as he opened his mouth to converse, any young lady would think, "What the fuck is this guy saying?"

Walsh continued to weave his way to his car and off he drove. He parked two blocks north of The Lyons' Den. The block was dark because of the absence of any street lights. Danny safely parked, but was overcome by drinking fatigue. He opened the driver and passenger windows with the intention of taking a short nap. The insufferable heat of the day gave way to a soft summer breeze. The breeze cooled Walsh's brow as he slowly slipped into dreamland.

He was enjoying the security and peace of a deep sleep, but it was only going to be a temporary state. All of a sudden, Walsh felt a sting. Unconsciously, he slapped his neck thinking he was shooing away a pesky mosquito. The penetrating pressure increased and Walsh awoke realizing that it was not an insect, but something more sinister. He was groggy no more. His eyes were as wide as possible.

Then words of dread, "Get the fuck out of the car, scumbag."

The pressure accosting his neck intensified. It was a stiletto knife. Walsh reached into his jeans front pocket collecting all his money.

He exited the car confronted by four youths. The knife wielder and his three buddies looked quite similar. Not one of them was over five-foot-nine and they weren't Irish. Walsh immediately brought up his right hand which contained 800 some odd dollars. He gave it to one of the youthful felons behind the stiletto king. When the money passed from one hand to the other,

Walsh felt a sharp object entering his upper torso followed by another stick of the stiletto, six inches lower. The first blow was quick as a mini-second. The second entered Walsh slowly, calculating, and twisting as if to exact the maximum pain. Danny, looked into the knife wielder's face. He saw a demented smile and eyes of glee. In other words, this scumbag was enjoying the shit out of this.

The third entry was in progress, but didn't extend fully into Walsh's body. Walsh changed from a slobbering drunk into an enraged lunatic. Although injured severely, he was now a street warrior and called upon his knowledge of past brawls.

He took the offense against this prick, blasting the skinny assassin with a left hook that jolted his head six inches to the rear. The blow forced the blades third intrusion to be no more than a pin prick. Danny threw a right cross that grazed the knife wielder, who was taking backwards steps. He turned with his three cohorts and started his retreat.

Walsh was now in full pursuit yelling, "You thought you were going to kill me, you cock sucker. I'm gonna kill you, you ball-less coward."

The gang was much too fast for Walsh so the short chase ended.

Danny looked down at his powder blue steamfitter shirt and saw it was drenched in blood. The summer humidity cause the blood to coagulate into separate gooey patterns upon the shirt. Danny lifted his shirt to find two incisions oozing blood in a slow methodical cadence. It wasn't going to stop and Walsh knew it. He made his way back to the car and like a chameleon, changed into a rational, sober person.

Walsh new his next stop had to be a hospital. Luckily, he only had to drive several blocks to Misericordia Hospital. As he drove, he was hunched over the steering wheel and it appeared that he was steering with his chin. The drive was only ten minutes. He parked to the right of the emergency room entrance. He got out of the car and walked with the stooped posture of an 80-year old man.

Danny entered the emergency room with both his hands pressed tightly on his wounds, hoping to halt the flow of blood. A young blonde nurse ran to his side and with the help of an orderly placed Walsh on a gurney. Immediately, another nurse affixed a needle in Danny's arm that was attached to a hanging bottle containing crystal clear fluid. Walsh was now in the safe confines of a hospital causing his stress level to decrease as a veil of calmness settled over his entire body.

It didn't last for long. As the doctor inspected his wounds, the older nurse who administered the needle casually asked Walsh his name. Danny's mental state had dual dimensions. On one side of his cranium he was rational enough to mentally assess his situation. On the other side it was time to assume an alias, seeing he didn't have health insurance.

Danny spouted out, "Jim Morrison!" in honor of the recently-deceased, rock celebrity.

The nurse asked for his social security number.

Walsh hesitated with a noticeable pause and blurted out, "072-35-3118".

The nurse had a quizzical look on her face. Walsh pinned her to be, "The Wicked Witch of the West" and she bared watching.

The male orderly chimed in, "Do you have any ID on you?"

Walsh shot back, "No, I don't have any ID, just patch me up."

Walsh wasn't aware that the question was posed because he was the victim of a crime.

Danny felt a raging heat within his body replacing his recent tranquil state. Yep, the other side of his thick head started to make inroads. Walsh's body temperature was rising.

The Wicked Witch equipped with clipboard and pen in hand, asked once again, "What is your first name and how do you spell Morrison?"

Walsh, fully agitated responded, "It's Jim Morrison, two r's and one s. Now can you stop with the questions and take care of these fucking stab wounds?"

Danny's elevated harshness didn't deter Witchy.

She continued as if she hadn't heard the last rant. "And what's your social security number, Mr. Morrison?" as she prepared to note it on the hospital admittance form.

It now became Mount Vesuvius time for Walsh.

He answered with a voice elevation one level below a scream. "You want my fucking social security number again, 072-37-3223."

"Well, Mr. Morrison, that's not the number you gave me the first time," responded Witchy.

Walsh screamed, "That's the fucking social security number they gave me when I went to the social security office."

Calmly, the Wicked Witch gave the reply that ignited a full blown eruption.

"Mr. Morrison, if that's your name, I do not believe you are being very truthful."

Walsh's face was pizza oven hot. He sat erect on the gurney.

At the same time ripped the needle from his arm as he screamed, "I am going to another fucking hospital."

He slowly turned to each of the four surrounding faces and bellowed out, "Fuck you. Fuck you. Fuck you."

When he got to the young nurse with the angelic face, he couldn't say "Fuck you" and he calmly said to her, "And you too."

Then he leapt from the gurney and, with revitalized energy, short stepped his way from the emergency room to his car.

When he entered his car Walsh lifted his shirt, and noticed the bleeding had picked up speed. He exited the hospital parking lot with the intent of driving five miles to Montefiore Hospital. He turned on the radio and listened to The Beatles' "Let It Be." He sang along as he made a left turn south onto Webster Avenue. He started to laugh uncontrollably.

Danny spoke to himself and in between laughing fits he proclaimed, "How lucky am I?" He looked down at the right side of his shirt, and thought "The cocksucker was a lefty. If he were a righty I'd be dead. The first stab would have hit me right in the heart."

Walsh mused to himself, "How come I don't have that luck with women or gambling?"

He continued south on Webster Avenue with the New York Central railroad tracks on his left and the thirty-foot stone wall defining the outer boundary of Woodlawn Cemetery on his right.

Danny quipped, "How ironic, Woodlawn Cemetery."

Suddenly, the situation turned grim. Danny was getting dizzy which was a harbinger of the immediate future. As dizziness overcame Walsh, he steered the car at a ninety degree angle into the stone wall. The speed was not that significant, so Danny suffered no additional injuries from the crash. The car was smoking because of a busted radiator. Walsh regained consciousness and realized he had a dilemma as this part of Webster Avenue was sparsely travelled. Danny, still bleeding, was comfortably drifting into what might become his last sleep.

His peaceful snore was interrupted by a commanding voice, "Son, you have to wake up."

Walsh responded to the voice and a gentle nudge. As he opened his eyes, he saw a six-foot uniformed police officer prodding him. Walsh heard an Irish brogue stating he was going to help him out of the car.

Danny blurted out, "I'm not going back to that fucking hospital."

The next words he heard would universally impress anyone in Walsh's situation, "Lad, in twenty minutes you won't need a hospital."

Walsh's ire towards Misericordia Hospital dissipated. With the gentle assistance of Officer McCallion, Danny was removed from his car.

In five minutes, he was in front of the emergency room entrance for the second time. Officer McCallion went in and returned with a gurney and the hospital orderly. Both men gingerly moved Walsh from the patrol car to the gurney. Danny, still in a groggy state, recognized the orderly as the same person he "Fuck you'd" previously. The two men ushered him into the emergency room and Walsh, feeling ashamed, saw the other three that he savagely insulted less than an hour ago.

Even though he thought he was bleeding to death, he knew he had to make things right. There he was, laying in a submissive state, looking into the eyes of all four again. Their faces denoted anger and fear. Anger because of Walsh's prior behavior and the fear of not knowing if this psycho would flip out again. Immediately, Danny set out to make amends.

First, "I'm sorry," to the doctor. The doctor gave Walsh a forgiving pat on the shoulder.

Next, "I'm sorry," to the orderly whose response was a shrug with a brother-to-brother wink.

Next, was nurse Witchy. Sheepishly, Walsh declared his apology and it was met with two eyes that showed no forgiveness.

If anything they emulated an intense dislike bordering on hate for Danny Boy.

Danny thought to himself, "Boy, this is one miserable bitch and if she's married, I feel sorry for the husband."

Walsh turned to angel face and his eyes were imploring forgiveness from her.

She sensed it and before he could offer his apology, she spoke softly with loving eyes. "You're forgiven, I know it was the drink and your injuries that made you ornery. We all have our bad days. Yours was more traumatic than most."

She shyly smiled as she removed Walsh's shirt. His eyes welled up. This moment of compassion and her face would become a life long memory for Danny. After his apologies, Walsh had to face the wicked one and fess up.

"My name is Daniel Walsh," and along with his address he revealed his real social security number.

The saline bottle was reattached and X-rays were taken.

Two detectives from the 47th precinct entered the emergency room as the X-rays were completed. Both men, one Irish and one Italian were imposing figures. They were both over six-feet tall, impeccably dressed, and sporting that no nonsense look about them. The interview lasted no more than ten minutes. As a result of Danny's drunken state, he could only give a vague description of the four assailants. He told the detectives that it would be a fifty-fifty shot to positively ID the four suspects. The detectives told

Danny to please contact them, if he could remember anything that would be pertinent to his case.

The attending doctor grinned as he returned with the x-rays, and he informed Walsh that none of the intrusions damaged his internal organs. He told Walsh that the only injury was to the right side of his rib cage.

"Mr. Walsh, your ribs have been badly bruised from the assault. When you resume a normal state, your ribs will be quite sore with pain when coughing, sneezing, heavy breathing and laughing. It won't be pleasant."

He knew what the doctor meant by normal state. He really meant sobered up. The doctor advised him to be still as possible and not aggravate the right side. He told him to sleep on his left side and no heavy lifting for a full month.

"We're going to keep you all day and possibly the entire weekend to make sure there are no complications."

The doctor left and the orderly transported Walsh to the third floor. When they approached the nurses' station, the orderly made a right turn and entered Room 301. Walsh knew the reason he was in this particular room, was so the staff could constantly have their eyes on a potential lunatic. The orderly helped him into the bed.

Danny asked, "What time is it?"

"6:15 a.m."

Walsh mused to himself, "Nine hours ago I was happy as a lark, money in my pocket and the pursuit of a fair maiden on my mind. Now I am broke, with life-threatening puncture wounds. That is surely one turn of events."

He was laying on his back and was slowly sobering up. The pain the doctor promised was making itself known. Danny informed the attending nurse and she returned with two pills that would diminish the hurting. The nurse was about his age, most likely Italian, with a beautiful olive complexion, dark intriguing eyes, and sporting a well formed figure. She was, however, not the same as angel face. Let's say she knew the ins and outs of life and you couldn't bullshit her.

She told him, "I've been told you're quite the character." She cracked a semi smile and continued, "Let me tell you Irish boy, you're not going to cause me any problems. Because if you do, I'll caress your right rib cage."

Walsh thought to himself, "Is this a hospital or a POW camp?" The Roman beauty softened a bit.

"Listen, I know you went through a horrible experience. One, that no human being should have to endure. But we can't help you, if you are going to carry on and curse at the staff. So you behave and I'll give you TLC, understand?"

She took Danny's temperature and checked his pulse and made sure the saline bottle was full. Her eyes attached to Danny's. She didn't say a word and tenderly stroked his forehead and hair.

Before she left, she continued still smiling, "Don't worry you thick mick, Elena is going to take care of you. You don't have a thing to worry about. You're safe."

She left the room and Walsh said to himself, "Wow, what a woman. Never in my life did I ever go from intense dislike to loving a person in ten minutes. She is the proverbial something else."

At eight a.m. who was staring down at him with his patented wacky demeanor, but Artie Willis. He was in yesterday's work clothes. His jet blacked hair sported that combed back greasy look with the left and right sides elongated sticking out like wings as if he was ready to take off. The carpenter-crack revealing position of his work jeans was a bit more pronounced than usual. The reason being a pint of Seagrams was protruding from his right rear pocket causing the pants to go further south.

Yep, there he was Sir Arthur, unshaven and vulgar as ever quipping, "What the fuck happened to you?" as he lit up a Camel.

Walsh responded sarcastically, "Artie, I'm so glad you asked. You see with this treacherous heat wave we've been working in, I decided to take off today and spend the weekend here. Here at Misericordia Hospital, I can enjoy a well deserved rest, servants at my command, and three five-star meals everyday.

"Listen, you fucking idiot. I was mugged, stabbed, humiliated, and rendered penniless. That's what the fuck happened to me."

Artie bobbed and weaved in a drunken state, took out his bottle of Seagrams and gulped down a three ounce blast.

"Well," Artie replied, "the neighborhood knows already. Buster got a call from Ray Quigley, who works in the 47th precinct.

Buster told me to visit you to find out what exactly happened. Boy, that's some appreciative attitude you have."

Danny sheepishly responded, "I'm sorry I barked at you Artie. I really appreciate you coming to visit."

Just then Elena came in and looked suspiciously at Artie who was lighting up his second Camel.

She took his vitals again. Just when she was adjusting his pillow with her back turned, Willis began a menacing movement which would eventually result in him pinching her in the ass.

Walsh yelled out, "No!"

Elena was startled and Artie retreated his right hand.

She exclaimed, "What's wrong?"

Walsh answered, as he viciously stared at Artie, "I must have moved too abruptly, I got a shooting pain in my ribs."

Elena gently chided him, "Any movement will bring pain, so be as still as possible."

She turned to leave and at the same time stared Artie down. She didn't like him. Danny realized he saved Artie from a verbal and possible physical beat down.

Walsh snapped at Artie, "Really? You were going to grab her ass. That's all I need is to have some wild eyed nurse seeking revenge because one, Arthur Willis, assaulted her behind. Sure, you leave, I pay."

Walsh lightened up and had that twinkle in his eye. He graciously thanked Artie for the visit and his concern.

Artie replied, "Take care, Danny Boy. I know I'm just the first of many visitors, so get yourself ready."

Artie turned and left, carpenter crack and all.

Elena's pills seemed to be working. He felt truly relaxed and eventually drifted off to sleep. The deep sleep lasted three hours and ended with a gentle nudge by Elena. It was vitals time. Everything was perfect and she told Walsh lunch was on its way. Since Danny's appetite had diminished, he took a look-and-see approach towards lunch.

As his thoughts drifted from food, in came Mickey O sporting a big smile. "How's it been mate? I heard you had a rough go of it. Here, I brought you something that will lighten your load." He opened a bakery box featuring an assortment of jelly donuts, black and white cookies and various types of crullers.

"Thanks, Mickey, I will devour these beauties when my appetite returns. Right now I'm just not hungry."

"Well, you'll enjoy them when you're ready. Geez, Danny I hate seeing you in this state. I only wish I knew who did this to you. Retribution would be extracted from them, believe me."

Responding in a low, weak tone Walsh said, "I know you have my back, Mickey. I just want this self-imposed guilt to fade away as soon as possible. I feel like a fool. As a matter of fact, I am a fool even though those scum bags messed me up. It's what I did prior that got me in this mess and I can only blame myself."

There was a five-second lull, after which Mickey gently responded, "Dan, we all suffer the shackles of embarrassment in our lives. Most are minor. Where you get loaded and say inappropriate things. The next day you may have to offer a few mea culpas. There's also times where you may have done something foolish, which travels throughout the neighborhood as an exaggerated fact. That situation casts a temporary veil over you, but in time it evaporates from the memories of all. In a crazy way, embarrassment is good for us."

Walsh looked quizzically at Mickey O, but remained silent.

Mickey continued, "Embarrassment and its twin shame, are always instigated and perpetrated on us, by guess who? The answer, us. It's always the result of our actions. The definitions of those actions vary in description and degree. The simple ones: being obnoxiously drunk, crashing your father's car, cheating on a test and being caught, etc. These situations are cleared from the guilt of your memory, with a sincere apology and in some cases minor disciplinary action. In the future, they may be brought up as self inflicted degradation by you saying, 'Look how much of a schmuck I was.' Thus making yourself the butt of the joke. Those are the embarrassments that one can easily remedy.

"However, there are situations, because of their nature, that haunt one's memory and creates a festering mental wound. For example, you said you'd help a friend who was in a time of need. Shortly after you tell the friend, you wish you could help, but there is nothing you could do. The facts were you could have helped, but you didn't want to commit to the effort and time needed. You have planted the tiny guilt seed within your brain. Now what happens?

Your friend's circumstances have gotten worse and you realize that your selfishly proclaimed inability to help added to your friend's distress. If you had rendered assistance, your friend's present situation may have been averted. Now unbeknownst to this friend, who believed you were truthful in you inability to assist him, the small guilt seed starts to flourish. You see, Danny, you knew you deserted your buddy. This guilt will intensify every time you see your friend. The guilt will remain with you for the rest of your life or until you develop dementia. So Daniel, any time you intentionally welch on a handshake deal or premeditate an environment which insults or humiliates a friend for your own amusement, you have planted that small seed.

"Now my son, you haven't risen to any degree of perpetrating deceit or humiliation on a friend. Did you make a mistake? Of course, you did. You just joined the many of us, who reaffirm the age old adage, we all make mistakes. It's just one of the measures that indicates that you are actually a human being.

"Listen Walshy, people care about you. Their first reaction will be humorous after learning all the intricacies of your tale of woe. But after the laughter, the universal concern will be, 'Will he be alright?' Dan, you are respected and loved. Don't forget that. That my boy, is the end of the sermon. Mass is over. Off to the gin mill we go."

Walsh cracked a big grin and a mild chuckle which caused him to grab at his right rib cage.

"Are you OK? Want me to get a nurse?"

"No," Walsh replied, "Every time I laugh or cough it settles painfully on my right side. Mickey, you really pumped up my spirits. You reaffirmed true friendship and what it entails. All those short tutorials given by you and guys like Buster, Duke, Neil, and Tom Flaherty, well all those lessons didn't fall on deaf ears. It's one of the reasons why I wouldn't wanted to have been born and raised in any other place. I love the neighborhood and all its characters."

Walsh's demeanor changed again. The realization of what he had experienced finally hit home. He was ninety-percent sober and inside he felt like shit. No matter how Mickey O attempted to lighten his load, he had an emotional volcano within himself and it erupted.

Walsh with tears streaming down his cheeks said, "Mickey, I'm a fucking idiot, I just wish I was at another place at another time."

Mickey O patted his friend on his head, "Listen buddy, just give it some time. After a month, this will be a memory. You'll muse to yourself and realize 'I've got a story to tell my children.' Please believe me Walshy, that's how it's going to end. Just give it time. Now I'm leaving. You just close your eyes, remove your inner burden, and drift off to a peaceful sleep."

Walsh smiled as he closed his eyes.

He heard Mickey O softly speaking again, "By the way, the two hundred you owe me from Tuesday nights Yankee game, take as much time as you want to pay me."

Walsh smiled and pondered, "After all the mush and sentimentality, Mickey O was still Mickey O." Walsh wouldn't want it any other way.

A therapeutic sleep did overtake Walsh. When he awoke he realized he was completely sober and the shame he felt had lessened a bit. Rationality was now part of the equation. Danny adopted the "Que sera sera" mantra, "What will be will be."

Walsh realized that his parents wouldn't be mad. He knew they would be relieved that their son was going to live. He knew his friends would bust his balls and joke about the incident. But Mickey O was right. After a months time, everything would be back to normal and that made Walsh smile.

While he was cleansing his inner spirit, an attendant came in with his dinner. Danny rang for the nurse. This time it wasn't Elena; she had gone home. Approaching his bed was a nurse, shy of fifty years old, raven black hair and exaggerated deep blue eyes, with all the features of a runway model. Walsh thought to himself, if I were fifty and she was single, there would definitely be a meeting of the minds. She was just one word, gorgeous. Walsh brought himself back to reality. After all she could be Danny's young mother.

The nurse spoke as if it were a rehearsed line.

"What's the problem boyo? Is it pain you're having?"

There she was, Irish as Irish could be. Danny thought she must have been a post WWII Irish import.

Danny smiled at his new friend and stated, "It's pain all right. The pain in one's heart when one casts his eyes on beauty in its perfect form."

The nurse blushed. "Oh, my God. Never did I think I'd be swept off my feet by one short declarative sentence. Much less by a young man who's a couple of years younger than my son."

She tried to stifle her smile, but her giggle gave it away. She was impressed by this dimpled-faced, one-line Casanova.

"I know you must have heard about my nastiness when I arrived, but I have made amends. It's the real Danny Walsh you are confronted with now. A young man with the flaws of youth, but one that doesn't have a mean spirited bone in his body. A person who will comply with all medical personnel, especially you, the love of one that I could never attain."

"Jesus, lad, how many love lies and moves do you have?"

Danny laughed and at the same time grasped his right side, as pain shot from his waist to his neck.

The smiling beauty turned serious and said, "Daniel, movements and laughter are going to bring pain, so remain calm and still as best you can. Let me readjust your pillow and tilt the bed on a slight angle."

Her gentleness was natural. Walsh knew she was beautiful on the inside as well as the outside. Danny saw the wall clock; it was 6:45 p.m.

"What's your name?"

"Claire Lavelle."

"Well, Claire Lavelle, I want to ask you a favor."

"What kind of favor?"

"Claire, could you get a wheelchair and bring me to a room that has a phone, so I could call my mother to let her know how I am doing. I know she must be a nervous wreck and I just want to assure her I'm all right."

Claire's eyes softened to a mother's concern.

"Well, Danny Boy, I'm not supposed to do this. Being a mother, I know it would lighten my heart to know my son was going to be OK."

"I appreciate the favor."

Claire shortly returned with a wheelchair and gently assisted Walsh from the bed to the chair. She brought him to an empty administrative office.

She told him, "I'll leave so you can have some privacy. Just wave to me when you are finished."

Danny voiced his thanks.

When Claire left he dialed Morrison's Bar. A voice answered. It was Billy Woods, a seldom used fill in for Mickey O.

"Billy, what's the line on the Yankees?"

"The Red Sox are favored 6/7." That meant if you wanted the Red Sox, you had to lay $7 to win $5. On the other hand betting the Yankees, you would lay $5 to win $6.

Without delay, Walsh said, "Gimme the Yankees, forty times getting the six."

Woods confirmed the bet and hung up. The conversation was all of 45 seconds.

Walsh had to pretend to be conversing with his mother, while holding the phone to his ear with no one on the listening end. He kept the phone this way for five minutes.

Then said in a loud tone that could be heard by Claire, "Don't worry Mom, I'll be all right. I have a lovely nurse taking care of me."

He hung up and motioned to Claire that he was finished.

Claire enters the office and said, "I'm so glad you called your mother. Now she can have a good nights sleep. I couldn't help but hear the last part of your conversation. Thank you for the compliment."

Walsh disguised his face of deceit and told Claire his mother thanked her for taking care of her boy.

"That's my job and I'm so glad your mother's mind is at ease."

Walsh's eyes could had given his lie away, but Claire didn't take notice.

She escorted Danny back to the room, assisted him back into bed and told him, "If you need me just signal."

After Claire left, the room started to fill, one by one, with a menagerie of crazed alcoholics of both sexes. Yes the invasion had begun. There was Dealy and McNeil carrying a large cooler of beer and after fifteen minutes the room was filled. Everyone laughing, drinking and smoking as if it were New Years Eve.

Sporadically, Walsh would get the, "How you feeling?"

"Were you stabbed or shot?"

"Did it hurt?"

"Did you lose a lot of blood?"

Followed by a self indulged request, "Do you mind if I sit at the edge of the bed?"

These people were there as if they were visiting a ghost. In their minds, it was just another excuse for a party. At least the girls, Rita Geary, Mary Connelly, and Jeannie Clarke held Walsh's hand and kissed him on his cheek showing their concern. The party continued and seemed as if it would never end. Twelve lunatics enjoying life to the fullest and Danny just laying still with his mouth open in amazement. The wall clock denoted nine. One by one, the group bid farewell, and compassionately voiced their concerns in hope of a speedy recovery.

He was by himself again. He realized that his friends cared for him and that bolstered his spirits. His mind was now at ease as he fell asleep. He awoke at 11:30 p.m., as if his mind was controlled by an alarm clock. He knew why. He had to know if the Yankees won. Signaling the nurse was the obvious move and Claire came with a concerned look.

"What's wrong, Danny?"

"Claire, I'm such an avid Yankees fan, I wonder if you knew if they won tonight?"

"Well, son I know not a thing about baseball, but I will ask one of the security guards."

She came back in ten minutes.

He was semi-conscious when he heard Claire's soothing voice, "Danny, the Yankees won."

He couldn't celebrate. Exhaustion had taken over and he blissfully returned to his dreams.

When morning arrived, Walsh opened his eyes, to see his old friend, Elena. Walsh smiled and was happy to see her._

"Good morning, Irishman. I see you had a good night's sleep. How are we feeling,?"

Still in a foggy state, Danny told her, "Elena, I feel better than yesterday. If all the tests and x-rays come back negative, I'm going to have to leave you today."

In a serious tone, Elena replied, "Listen kiddo, you still need medical care. It Isn't like you had your tonsils removed and we send you home with a quart of ice cream."

Walsh interrupted, "My dear, I know you want the best for me and you are a person one cannot bullshit. So here's the rub. I can't afford to stay here. In other words, 'I got no bread, Ned.'"

Elena was still concerned, "Danny, the doctors have to make sure there are no complications and that could take a couple of days."

"No can do!" was Walsh's reply.

Elena's face told the story. There was no way her boy was going to stay.

"Danny, you have to sign a few papers confirming that you want to be released from Misericordia Hospital."

"Bring them on. I'll sign whatever you want. By the way, could you bring me to a phone. I have to call two people to take me home before they charge me for another day."

Elena brought him to the nurses station and he called Matty Kirby and Brian Lynch. Both said they would be there within the hour. Walsh thanked his buddies and told Elena he was finished with the calls.

He saw a semi cold breakfast by his bed when he arrived back to his room.

Pointing to the breakfast he asked, "Elena, does this meal mean I will be charged for another day?"

"No, you'll be charged for this day at noon. So if your boys pick you up before then, there will be no additional charges. I'll make sure the needed papers are here within the hour. You'll sign them. Your buddies will come and off you'll go with time to spare."

Walsh was now at ease. His mind began to wander as he picked at the scrambled eggs. He knew his father and mother were more worried than they ever had been about their son. The shame of a drunken fool could not be completely erased from his mind. He used the mental crutch of Mickey O's credo, that time would erase the awkwardness and shame of the present. He worried that he may not ring the time bell for the Monday morning shapeup at the steamfitters shanty. Realizing that his mind was spinning with worry, he calmed his emotions by prayer.

Danny wasn't a card carrying Catholic, but he did the required Christmas and Easter obligations. The Sunday Masses were eliminated by screaming Bloody Mary in the morning hangovers. This time of solitude allowed him to reflect. During this veil of peace, he meditated mind to mind with his Lord. For a thirty second period, he was an emotional wreck. His eyes welled and his body shook uncontrollably. He silently spoke to his Savior and offered a life long contrition. His worries melted like the Spring snow. Adherence to Mickey O's philosophy and his newly acquired dispensation from Jesus enabled Danny to smile.

Elena arrived, "Don't we look like the happy one? Did one of your girlfriends visit while I was gone and said you might get lucky this weekend?"

"Ha! Ha! Aren't we Alice Kramden? If you want to know, I had a powerful inward reflection which made me realize everyone screws up. I'm going to be all right."

Danny's response put a smile on her face as she said, "You know Irishman, you're starting to grow on me. I must admit I prefer the Dean Martin type, but a wild man like you could persuade me otherwise. What the hell am I saying? That's all I need is some drinking lunatic in my life!"

They both broke out in laughter.

When the laughter subsided, Elena's sincerity rose to the occasion again.

"I know our paths crossed for only a short time and we will probably never meet again. There's something I see in you. I see a kind, loving, compassionate person. It's just the inner wildness you need to control. However, my brief observance of you, unfortunately confirms you will always be the wild Colonial boy. So Daniel, go forth and enjoy life to the fullest." Elena gently kissed Danny on the cheek as she whispered, "Maybe we'll meet in the next life."

Danny squeezed Elena's hand and said, "I guess what you said was meant to be complimentary, so thank you. Elena, when I reflect on this many years from now, I'll have this one emotion. It will be the memory of you. Because without you, I don't know if I would have fully healed mentally and physically. You'll always have a tiny spot in the inner sanctum of my heart and that's beautiful because I will always be able to envision your loving face."

"Stop it, Mr. Mick. You're raising my body temperature," said Elena as she loosened the grasp of their hands.

As she turned to leave, she gave a last smile, "I must visit the rest of my patients now."

Danny wanted to emblazon her face into his mind because he would never see it again.

The hulking figures of Matty Kirby and Brian Lynch appeared.

They both asked, "What happened to you?"

Walsh sarcastically replied, "As I was leaving Yonkers Raceway I tripped and fell on a stiletto knife."

"Really?" said Brian.

Danny aggravated, replied, "The both of you are prime examples of the effects of overconsumption of alcohol on the brain.

Listen, you bird brains. I was stabbed after being relieved of all my money and now I just want to get the hell out of here."

After five seconds of silence, Danny continued, "I'm sorry for being such an obnoxious asshole, but it hasn't been easy these last couple of days. You guys are the greatest and you'll never know how much I appreciate this."

Congenial smiles radiated on all three mens faces. The head nurse came in with the appropriate paperwork accompanied by an orderly with a wheelchair. Danny signed all the designated spaces.

The orderly and Kirby helped him into the wheelchair. A shooting pain encompassed his whole right rib section.

Walsh screamed, "Holy shit!"

The head nurse responded, "Not exactly; it's the unpleasant after effects of your injury. So don't move in any way that favors your right side."

Walsh thought, "Now she tells me! What a condescending, elitist bitch. Another incident of oil and vinegar."

Uncaringly, she continued, "The doctor has given you medication for the pain. Your nurse bandaged your wounds and here are replacement bandages that should last you for a week or so."

Her indifferent attitude hastened Walsh's desire to exit the premise as fast as possible. Lynch understood Danny's wishes and gave the attendant a fiver. So, there it was Danny zooming along with Kirby and Lynch following in a trot.

Danny spotted angel face. He turned in her direction and with his eyes silently apologized. This muted apology must have been interpreted for that short stare resulted in angel face blowing a kiss in Danny's direction. That was the finale. Walsh, was in a weird way, sad to leave. Angel face put a stamp on everything that had occurred. Danny learned so much from the assault on him and realized that he was a complete asshole before, during, and immediately after the incident. This incident emphasized the deeper side of life. He was able to be the recipient of human compassion.

From the lifesaving arrival of an Irish cop to the care of the medical staff who helped to stabilize him, these experiences left an indelible mark on him. The nurses, angel face, the Irish beauty, and Elena treated him as if he were their own son or brother. These ladies brought out a newly formed religiosity that had laid dormant in his soul. They revived what was always innate in his being. They were sterling examples of how we all should treat each other. The compassion, love and empathetic care that one stranger could show for another was amazing.

Lynch had his car parked ten feet from the front entrance. When they exited, Walsh was hit with a blast of heat and humidity which sucked away his breath. The short walk to the car, even with the help of Kirby and Lynch, was difficult for Danny. Walsh knew he had been dealt a near knock-out blow. His youthful strength had been diminished to that of an elderly man. It was his youth that had saved him from crossing over to the other side. Lynch and Kirby gently helped Danny into the passenger seat.

The ride back to the neighborhood was only a twenty minute trek. Conversation was monopolized by both friends voicing their concern for him and trivial local gossip that had evolved in the short time Danny was hospitalized. The car reached its final destination which was a parking spot right outside Walsh's walkup apartment house.

The two six-footers assisted Danny to his feet. Even though they were very gentle, Walsh felt the discomfort in his right side. Danny lifted his clean shirt and noticed blood splotches on the dressing Elena affixed. Walsh knew that this ordeal was far from over. He asked Brian if he had the bag with new bandages and pain pills. Brian nodded in the affirmative.

"Well boys, this isn't going to be pleasant, but step by step we'll go."

Step by step it was, as they made it up the court yard steps and three flights, with Danny grimacing all the way. After what seemed to be the length of a boring baseball game, they were in front of apartment 3G.

The friends tapped lightly at the door and heard steps approaching. The door opened and there stood Mrs. Walsh, ashen white.

With a trembling voice softly stated, "Danny, you made it back to me."

Mr. Walsh was behind Danny's mom and said, "Don't worry, Mother, we'll take care of this lad."

As the two assistants entered the apartment, they observed the three gently hugging each other.

Matty Kirby said, "Our job is done, Daniel. Let the healing begin," as both men left the apartment.

Mae Walsh assisted her son to his bed and removed his old bandages. The wounds were still raw. Mae applied the antiseptic ointment and replaced the bandage with the loving care only a mother could administer.

"Danny, I have your favorite stew on the stove waiting for you. I'll have it here within a minute."

Mae came back with a tray of stew and warm buttered bread. She propped Danny's head up with two additional pillows and watched Danny devour the stew. After a few minutes, she took an empty tray back to the kitchen and said, "Sleep my son, if you need me just call."

Walsh drifted off and didn't wake up until Sunday morning.

Mae heard her son's movements and went to the kitchen. She prepared a butter-smeared, day-old scone and a pot of hot tea. She entered his room and saw a young man with a face of sorrow.

"Ma, I'm sorry I hurt you and dad. I'm not proud of myself and I hate the fact that I brought shame to our family. I'm a fool and my selfish actions have caused such anguish and pain."

Mae replied sternly, "Danny I never want to hear those words again. You are my son and you have qualities and traits others would envy. You've been nothing but a blessing since the day you were born. Sure, when I got you home from the hospital I saw that devilish look in your eyes. I said to myself, this one bears watching. That devilish look was real and revealed your unique nature and personality. Danny, you're not like the crowd. You march to your own tune, but that doesn't diminish from your personality. Your loyalty and love for you family and friends is the moral compass ingrained in you."

"You know son, God has a sense of humor, He embraces people like you. He realizes everyone has faults. In many instances those short comings can be used for outright evil purposes. Danny, you don't have an evil bone in your body and Our Lord knows that. Even though you may feel you are going through the lowest point in your life, God is actually chuckling. He knows how you're going to get out of this jam. His laughter is good natured and loving. He sees that at the end of the tunnel, His boy Danny will learn lessons for the good not the evil. He knows the results of your knock down will intensify your empathy and compassion for others. For the time being, He may be amused, but He is proud that one of His many earthly sons has taken a minor tragedy and made himself a better person."

Danny was almost knocked out of his bed. His mother's words attacked his psyche. It lifted any guilt or shame that he had. It was a mother's love talking, but it was also insightful. His mother made him realized he was loved. Danny turned to the tea and scone and quickly demolished both. His eyes began to droop and he drifted off to la-la land.

The TLC continued for all of Sunday until six a.m. Monday. Danny awoke without his mother's sweet voice that it was time to get up. She hadn't bothered him because she thought he had no intentions to go to work because of his injuries.

"Ma," Danny beckoned as he peeked into his parents bedroom, "I'm getting up to go to work, could you make me some bacon and eggs, please? After I take a shower, I'll need you to change my bandage. Thanks mom."

Mae knew her son and it would be a futile attempt to change his mind.

"All right my love, breakfast is on its way and I'll get the bandages and antibiotic ointment ready."

Danny gently cleansed the wound in the shower and noticed the hot water eliminated the crusted protection of his wounds which created a slight blood flow from the stilettos intrusion. That condition was minor, but when he touched his right side, it was still extremely painful. As he carefully dried off, he saw his mother had his work clothes on a hanger waiting for him.

While dressing, the shame and self guilt he had felt was diminishing. Now it was only the physical discomfort. There was still one hurdle he still had to leap over: the meeting with his boss Buster Reilly within the hour. Danny desperately needed the money and his physical inability to work placed him in a precarious position. Buster was one person you couldn't bullshit. He was a fair man who demanded one-hundred-percent effort. That thought weighed on his mind as he was finishing breakfast.

The doorbell rang. Danny got up from the kitchen table and opened the door to see Moose Morano and Artie Willis standing there. He kissed his mother and thanked her for breakfast. Moose and Artie noticed how Danny carefully negotiated the three flights of stairs. As they went to assist him, he waived them off and slowly descended the stairs without any help.

Once outside, Walsh was assaulted again by the perpetual heat wave. It had no quit in it. The ride to the construction site was quiet which enabled Danny to contemplate each scenario that might occur from the decision Buster would make about his future employment.

They parked right in front of the construction entrance and the three walked into the four-story building. They entered the steam fitters shanty. Buster was by himself, a cigarette dangling from his mouth, intently studying the days plans. He slowly raised his head after the rest of the crew assembled. He made mental notes of who was to do what. Walsh had maneuvered to the rear of the crew attempting to hide from Buster's vision.

Danny knew the jig was up when Buster said, "Walsh, what the hell are you doing here?"

Anyone who knows Buster realizes that question could be interpreted in various ways. It floats between condemnation and compassion. Walsh was in no man's land.

"Buster, I'm here to work. I need to work. Don't worry, I'll perform."

Buster's face softened which was a good sign, "Listen Walsh, I have to lay someone off and that someone is you."

Danny's read of Buster was apparently wrong.

"Our work is winding down here so you have to go."

Danny's face was ashen white and his inner being trembled as he heard the verdict.

Buster wasn't finished. "Danny, I'm going to carry you on paper for three weeks. Is that OK with you?"

Buster broke into a wide grin with an accompanying wink. Walsh was ecstatic. Buster's largess would ease Walsh's financial burdens. All he had to attend to was his physical well being.

Buster directed Artie to drive Walsh home saying, "Danny, stay home and mend. The next three Thursdays, I'll have one of the boys bring your money to the apartment."

Danny wanted to push his way through the crew and give Buster a big hug. His mind dismissed that idea. A tiny voice said, "If you hug this man, he'll blast you with a right hook." Walsh obliged the voice. A firm hand shake would do.

The ride home wasn't as somber as the one going to work. It was riddled with humor with Willis throwing multiple jabs at Danny. All of them with the same theme, "Walsh was an asshole."

Danny smiled and laughed, even though the laughter brought pain; it was a good pain. For Danny was now sky high and thanked Artie when they arrived at Walsh's apartment house. Artie grabbed Walsh's neck and brought Danny's head to his.

"Daniel, we were all worried about you. I'm so glad you came back to us. It would have been a razor cut to the neighborhoods heart if you had left us." Artie patted Walsh on the cheek and said, "Go get better. I'll be by on Thursday with your money."

Danny entered the apartment and Mae queried, "What happened, Danny?"

Walsh replied with a smile, "Mom, I got laid off."

Mae's face was dismayed.

"What?" she inquired.

Danny told her what had happened.

She smiled and said, "Son, that's how the people from our neighborhood are. They know how it is to be down on your luck, because they've been there. They don't voice charity. They perform charity with nothing, but a thank you in return. God bless Mr. Reilly."

Walsh wondered how this lady was so wise. His mother always amazed him and he now knew how a woman so loving could be so intuitive.

12
Gratitude

Twenty days later, Walsh took to his Saturday bartending duties. He was whole and went to bed knowing it was over. Mickey O was right. Time would be the healer.

On Sunday morning, he awoke to his mother urging him to the phone.

The voice he heard was Tom Flaherty. "Danny, I've been hot betting sports, so I'm going to take a hiatus from The Widow's Walk. I'd like you to take my shifts. You'd be doing me a favor."

Walsh replied, "Tom, you're doing me the favor. Buster's generous pay extension is about to run its course, so taking your shifts would help me out greatly. Thank you so much. I know you are doing this to help me out."

Flaherty responded, "Well, isn't that a coincidence. My hot streak and you needing work, just happened to coincide. The Lord does work in mysterious ways." As the conversation ended, Flaherty gave out one of his patented belly laughs, "Go get 'em Danny Boy."

Walsh hung up the phone and reflected on the last month. He was emotionally attacked once again. His drunken idiocy that had caused upheaval in his life was actually a lesson of the human spirit that he would never forget. He couldn't comprehend the fact that so many people truly cared about him and his well being. The stabbing unveiled the intricacies of love: from the care in the hospital to the love shown to him by his family and friends. By working Tom's shifts while his parents let him skate for two months rent, Danny became financially secure. He was able to pay off his hospital bills.

Tom called the house again to tell Danny he was coming back to work. Once again, fate was kind. The week before, Ralph Ward had rehired Danny as a truck driver because his business had taken a positive turn in the last three months. He would start when Flaherty came back to work. Walsh was amazed at all these so called coincidences, from Buster, to Tom, to Ralph, all in perfect harmony. All these acts of charity were put neatly into a box with a bow on top.

Flaherty invited Walsh to the clubhouse at Yonkers Raceway. He wanted to show his gratitude to Danny for working his shifts. That Friday night was unforgettable. Flaherty was dressed to the nines wearing a charcoal-grey suit, a light-blue tie that accentuated his vivid blue eyes, and a white carnation in his lapel. Walsh was underdressed with a black golf shirt and khaki pants. They enjoyed Martinis, shrimp cocktails, followed by two filet mignons and ended with dessert, coffee and Marie Brizard Anisette. During the entire meal, Walsh ran to the windows with their bets.

After the last race, Danny was a small loser and Tom was a small winner. Tom ordered more coffee and two anisettes while the crowd dissipated and the traffic diminished. The club house was empty as they left the building. Danny was ready to shake Tom's hand to thank him.

Before he could Tom spoke, "Danny, do me a favor and drive me home. Take my car and use it for the weekend and pick me up Monday evening."

Danny's eyes lit up as he saw the latest Lincoln model, white in color and absolutely gorgeous. He couldn't believe he would be driving this car for three days.

"Tom, I'll take care of this beauty, don't worry."

"Don't worry about taking care of the car, just enjoy it."

Walsh smiled as they arrived at Tom's car and Flaherty gave him the keys. On the drive home they talked about the night's races and what could have been, "If." That's the usual credo from confirmed horse bettors, "What if?"

They arrived at Tom's house and Danny turned and looked at Tom. Danny stared almost too long which would have made Flaherty uncomfortable.

The short silence was broken when Danny said, "Tom, there are no words which could express the magnitude of my appreciation of what you have done for me."

Tom quickly responded, "Daniel you're a fine lad. You treat people with respect and it's noticed. World War II guys were raised to be tough, but we always showed compassion in times of need. We can spot a phony immediately and we just ignore or steer away from him. Dan, you're genuine and that's the best compliment one can receive. You should consider all the solid, older guys in your

life as being street fathers. We attempt to mentor you lovable,
young lunatics to adhering to the moral rights and wrongs of life.
We hope them do's and don't's take hold and you pass that
philosophy on to your children. It's really that simple. Danny,
you're going to encounter many scum bags in your life. Don't
despair because you have friends, family and the neighborhood
coupled with a blue collar morality to fall back on. No, Danny,
don't thank me, instead I thank you for being a good friend that I
was able to assist during a difficult time."

With that said, Walsh firmly grasped Tom's hand and
thanked him again.

"I'm such a blessed person to have people like you in my
life."

Tom got out of the car. As he was opening the front door of
his house, he turned and gave a closing wave with his infamous
wink.

Walsh proceeded from the suburban part of the Bronx back
to the apartment and row houses surrounding Webster Avenue.
There was hardly any traffic as he drove home which enabled him
to be immersed in deep thought. In this moment of solitude he
examined his life from childhood to the present. He revisited the
sadness, humor, and compassion. The people he cherished and
lionized would leave this earthly realm way before him. During
this short ride, they were still here implementing their life lessons
and brandishing their loving mentoring spirit. He felt joy pierce his
being.

He reflected on the fact that there were many who were raised in the realm of abundance with lovely houses, expensive schooling. The one thing they couldn't have was the gritty love that the neighborhood fostered.

Their world lacked noisy over-crowded conditions. Their world knew nothing of not having the material pleasures. Their world didn't force them to make a stand. They didn't have to face the fact that even though you were going to take the worst of it, you couldn't back down. Their material largesse shielded them from receiving charity.

Charity in the neighborhood abounded. When someone was in need, it was addressed.

Walsh chided himself. These upper class people weren't bad or immoral. He knew they were decent. God didn't hold them in contempt for their success. They will get to the pearly gates the same as the Webster Avenue crew.

Danny mused, they would enjoy eternal joy, but for the neighborhood, well, Our Lord has set up a different heavenly experience. He'd tell St. Peter to direct the Saint Brendan's parishioners to the southwest area of Paradise where they would notice a replica of the neighborhood. Same houses, same addresses, however the changes would be noticed immediately. Each apartment would have air conditioning, not cross ventilation. There would be no more continuous noise; it would be quiet and peaceful. Shrimp cocktail and filet mignon whenever desired, accompanied by the finest wine and spirits. The bars would be exactly the same. The ball busting would be abundant with no offense taken. Everyday, there would be a luxurious bus transporting horse players to and from the tracks. There would always be all inclusive trips to various sections of Paradise. Celestial abundance and beauty would be there for the asking. Any pleasure in heaven would be there to enjoy. Danny pondered, even with all this opulence available, the people of the neighborhood would stay there ninety percent of their time.

His mind still raced when he was parking the car on Webster Avenue. How could his neighborhood be so impactful on his life while the world had so much more to give. He harkened to the recent past and what it had taught him. It made him realize the importance of his existence in this small parcel of land. He now knew why he had this intense, passionate love for this one particular part of this earth. He admired a piece of real-estate that could have such a dominating hold on each resident within its boundaries. It was truly remarkable. As Walsh entered his apartment, a final thought invaded his mind.

"God bless America, God bless all my family and friends, and God bless the neighborhood."

TALES FROM THE WIDOW'S WALK

DANNY HOFER

Acknowledgments

I would like to thank Tom Bessoir, who is a friend of mine from the poker world. Without his editorial prowess, this book would not be whole. Thank you.

Finally to my dear friend, "The Duke." You are missed by all. Rumors say that Heaven hasn't been the same since your arrival. I can only imagine. Rest in peace and laughter, especially the latter.

DANNY HOFER

About the Author

Danny Hofer was born and raised in his beloved "The Bronx." After two years in the U.S. Army, he attended St. John's University and earned his B. A. degree in 1971. In the early 80's, he completed graduate studies at Fordham University and received an M. B. A.

He is proud to be a retiree of the New York Police Department. He was lucky enough to have been assigned to the 44th Precinct for most of his career.

Made in the USA
Middletown, DE
28 March 2020

87404785R00129